Richard Doddridge Blackmore

Clara Vaughan

A novel. Vol. 1

Richard Doddridge Blackmore

Clara Vaughan
A novel. Vol. 1

ISBN/EAN: 9783337149536

Printed in Europe, USA, Canada, Australia, Japan

Cover: Foto ©Andreas Hilbeck / pixelio.de

More available books at **www.hansebooks.com**

CLARA VAUGHAN.

A NOVEL.

IN THREE VOLUMES.

VOL. I.

London and Cambridge:
MACMILLAN AND CO.
1864.

CLARA VAUGHAN.

BOOK I.

CHAPTER I.

I DO not mean to describe myself. Already I feel that the personal pronoun will appear too often in these pages. Knowing the faults of my character almost as well as my best friends know them, I shall attempt to hide them no more than would those beloved ones. Enough of this: the story I have to tell is strange, and short as my own its preamble.

The day when I was ten years old began my serious life. It was the 30th of December, 1842; and proud was the kiss my loving father gave me for spelling, writing, and pronouncing the date in English, French, and Italian. No very wonderful feat, it is true, for a clever child well-taught; but I was by no means a clever child; and no one except my father could teach me a single letter. When, after several years of wedlock, my parents found new joy in me, their bliss was soon overhung with care. They feared, but durst not own the fear, lest the wilful, passionate, loving creature, on whom their hearts were wholly set, should be torn from their love to a distance greater than the void of death; in a word, should prove insane. At length they could no longer hide this terror from each other. One look told it all; and I vaguely remember my hazy wonder at the scene that followed. Like a thief, I came from the corner behind the curtain-loops, and trembled at my father's knee, for him to say something to me. Then frightened at his silence—a thing unknown to me—I pulled his hands from before his eyes, and found hot tears upon them. I coaxed him then, and petted him, and felt his sorrows through me; then made believe to scold him for being so naughty as to cry. But I could not get his trouble from him, and he seemed to watch me through his kisses.

Before I had ceased to ponder dreamily over this great wonder, a vast event (for a child of seven) diverted me. Father, mother, and Tooty—for so I then was called—were drawn a long way by horses with yellow men upon them: from enlarged experience I infer that we must have posted to London. Here, among many marvels, I remember especially a long and mysterious interview with a kind, white-haired old gentleman, who wore most remarkable shoes. He took me upon his lap, which seemed to me rather a liberty; then he smoothed down my hair, and felt my head so much that I asked if he wanted to comb it, having made up my mind to kick if he dared to try such a thing. Then he put all sorts of baby questions to me which I was disposed to resent, having long discarded Cock Robin and Little Red-riding-hood. Unconsciously too, I was moved by Nature's strong hate of examination. But my father came up, and with tears in his eyes begged me to answer everything. Meanwhile my mother sat in a dark corner, as if her best doll was dying. With its innate pugnacity, my hazy intellect rose to the situation, and I narrowly heeded everything.

"Now go, my dear," the old gentleman said at last; "you are a very good little girl indeed."

"That's a great lie," I cried; for I had learned bad words from a flighty girl, taken rashly as under-nurse.

The old gentleman seemed surprised, and my mother was dreadfully shocked. My father laughed first, then looked at me sadly; and I did what he expected, I jumped into his arms. At one word from him, I ran to the great physician, and humbly begged his pardon, and offered him my very dearest toy. He came up warmly, and shook my father's hand, and smiled from his heart at my mother.

"Allow me, Mrs. Vaughan—allow me, my dear sir—to congratulate you cordially. The head is a noble and honest one. It is the growth of the brain that causes these little commotions; but the congestion will not be permanent. The fits, that have so alarmed you, are at this age a good symptom; in fact, they are Nature's remedy. They may last for seven years, or even for ten; of course they will not depart at once. But the attacks will be milder, and the intervals longer, when she has turned fourteen. For the intellect you need have no fear whatever. Only keep her quiet, and never force her to learn. She must only learn when it comes as it were with the wind. She will never forget what she *does* learn."

Hereupon, unless I am much mistaken, my father and mother fell to and kissed and hugged one another, and I heard a sound like sobbing; then they caught me up, and devoured me, as if I were born anew; and staring round with great childish eyes, I could not catch the old gentleman's glance at all.

Henceforth I learned very little, the wind, perhaps, being unfavourable; and all the little I did learn came from my father's lips. His patience with me was wonderful; we spent most of the day together, and when he was forced to leave me, I took no food until he returned. Whenever his horse was ordered, Miss Clara's little grey pony began to neigh and to fidget, and Miss Clara was off in a moment to get her blue riding-skirt. Even when father went shooting or fishing, Tooty was sure to go too, except in the depth of winter; and then she was up at the top of the house, watching all round for the gun-smoke.

Ah, why do I linger so over these happy times—is it the pleasure of thinking how fondly we loved one another, or is it the pain of knowing that we can do so no more?

Now, the 30th of December was my parents' wedding-day, for I had been born six years exact after their affectionate union. And now that I was ten years old—a notable hinge on the door of life—how much they made, to be sure, of each other and of me! At dinner I sat in glory between them, upsetting all ceremony, pleasing my father, and teasing my mother, by many a childish sally. So genial a man my father was that he would talk to the servants, even on state occasions, quite as if they were human beings. Yet none of them ever took the smallest liberty with him, unless it were one to love him. Before dessert, I interred my queen doll, with much respect and some heartache, under a marble flag by the door, which had been prepared for the purpose. My father was chief-mourner, but did not cry to my liking, until I had pinched him well. After this typical good-bye to childhood, I rode him back to the dining-table, and helped him and my mother to the last of the West's St. Peter grapes, giving him all the fattest ones. Then we all drank health and love to one another, and I fell to in earnest at a child's delight. Dearest father kept supplying me with things much nicer than are now to be got, while my mother in vain pretended to guard the frontier. It was the first time I tasted Guava jelly ; and now, even at the name, that scene is bright before me. The long high room oak-panelled, the lights and shadows flickering as on a dark bay horse, the crimson velvet curtains where the windows were gone to bed, the great black chairs with damask cushions, but hard and sharp at the edge, the mantel-piece all carved in stone which I was forbidden to kick, the massive lamp that never would let me eat without loose clouds of hair dancing all over my plate, and then the great fire, its rival, shuddering in blue flames at the thought of the frost outside; all these things, and even the ticking of the timepiece, are more palpable to me now than the desk on which I write. My father sat in his easy chair, laughing and joking, full of life and comfort, with his glass of old port beside him, his wife in front, and me, his " Clari-crops," at his knee. More happy than a hundred kings, he wished for nothing better. At one time, perhaps, he had longed for a son to keep the ancient name, but now he was quite ashamed of the wish, as mutiny against me. After many an interchange, a drink for father, a sip for Tooty, he began to tell wondrous stories of the shots he had made that day; especially how he had killed a woodcock through a magpie's nest. My mother listened with playful admiration; I with breathless interest, and most profound belief.

Then we played at draughts, and fox and goose, and pretended even to play at chess, until it was nine o'clock, and my hour of grace expired. Three times

Ann Maples came to fetch me, but I would not go. At last I went submissively at one kind word from my father. My mother obtained but a pouting kiss, for I wanted to wreak some vengeance; but my father I never kissed with less than all my heart and soul. I flung both arms around his neck, laid my little cheek to his, and whispered in his ear that I loved him more than all the world. Tenderly he clasped and kissed me, and now I am sure that through his smile he looked at me with sadness. Turning round at the doorway, I stretched my hands towards him, and met once more his loving, laughing eyes. Once more and only once. Next I saw him in his coffin, white and stark with death. By-and-by I will tell what I know; at present I can only feel. The emotions— away with long words—the passions which swept my little heart, with equal power rend it now. Long I lay dumb and stunned at the horror I could not grasp. Then with a scream, as in my fits, I flung upon his body. What to me were shroud and shell, the rigid look and the world of awe? Such things let step-children fear. Not I, when it was my father.

CHAPTER II.

How that deed was done, I learned at once, and will tell. By whom and why it was done, I have given my life to learn. The evidence laid before the coroner was a cloud and fog of mystery. For days and days my mother lay insensible. Then, for weeks and weeks, she would leap from her bed in fits of terror, stare, and shriek and faint. As for the servants, they knew very little, but imagined a great deal. The only other witnesses were a medical man, a shoemaker, and two London policemen. The servants said that, between one and two in the morning, a clear, wild shriek rang through the house. Large as the building was, this shriek unrepeated awoke nearly all but me. Rushing anyhow forth, they hurried and huddled together at the head of the great staircase, doubting what to do. Some said the cry came one way, some another. Meanwhile Ann Maples, who slept with me in an inner room at the end of a little passage, in the courage of terror went straight to her master and mistress. There, by the light of a dim night-lamp, used to visit me, she saw my mother upright in the bed, and pointing towards my father's breast. My father lay quite still; the bed-clothes were smooth upon him. My mother did not speak. Ann Maples took the lamp, and looked in her master's face. His eyes were open, wide open as in amazement, but the surprise was death. One arm was stiff around his wife, the other lax upon the pillow. As she described it in West-country phrase, "he looked all frore." The woman rushed from the room, and screamed along the passage. The servants ran to her, flurried and haggard, each afraid to be left behind. None except the butler dared to enter. Whispering and trembling they peered in after him, all ready to run away. Thomas Henwood loved his master dearly, being his foster-brother. He at once removed the bed-clothes, and found the fatal wound. So strongly and truly was it dealt, that it pierced the centre of my dear father's heart. One spot of blood and a small three-cornered hole was all that could be seen. The surgeon, who came soon after, said that the weapon must have been a very keen and finely-tempered dagger, probably of foreign make. The murderer must have been quite cool, and well acquainted with the human frame. Death followed the blow on the instant, without a motion or a groan. In my mother's left hand strongly clutched was a lock of long, black, shining hair. A curl very like it, but rather finer, lay on my father's bosom. In the room were no signs of disorder, no marks of forcible entrance.

One of the maids, a timid young thing, declared that soon after the stable-clock struck twelve, she had heard the front balusters creak; but as she was known to hear this every night, little importance was attached to it. The coroner paid more attention to the page (a sharp youth from London), who, being first in the main corridor, after the cry, saw, or thought he saw, a moving figure, where the faint starlight came in at the oriel window. He was the more believed, because he owned that he durst not follow it. But no way of escape could be discovered there, and the eastern window was strongly barred betwixt the mullions. No door, no window was anywhere found open.

Outside the house, the only trace was at one remarkable spot. The time had been chosen well. It was a hard black frost, without, as yet, any snow. The ground was like iron, and an Indian could have spied no trail. But at this one spot, twenty-five yards from the east end of the house, and on the verge of a dense shrubbery, a small spring, scarcely visible, oozed among the moss. Around its very head, it cleared, and kept, a narrow space quite free from green, and here its margin was a thin coat of black mineral mud, which never froze. This space, at the broadest, was but two feet and ten inches across from gravel to turf, yet now it held two distinct footprints, not of some one crossing and re-crossing, but of two successive steps leading from the house into the shrubbery. These footprints were re-markable; the one nearest the house was of the left foot, the other of the right. Each was the impression of a long, light, and pointed boot, very hollow at the instep. But they differed in this—the left footprint was plain and smooth, without mark of nail, or cue, or any other roughness; while the right one was clearly stamped in the centre of the sole with a small rectan-gular cross. This mark seemed to have been made by a cruciform piece of metal, or some other hard substance, inlaid into the sole. At least, so said a shoemaker, who was employed to examine it; and he added that the boots were not those of the present fashion, what he called "duck's bills" being then in vogue. This man being asked to account for the fact of the footprints being so close together, did so very easily, and with much simplicity. It was evident, he said, that a man of average stature, walking rapidly, would take nearly twice that distance in every stride; but here the verge of the shrubbery, and the branches striking him in the face, had suddenly curtailed the step. And to this, most likely, and not to any hurry or triumph, was to be ascribed the fact that one so wily and steadfast did not turn back and erase the dangerous tokens. Most likely, he did not feel what was beneath his feet, while he was battling with the tangle above.

Be that as it may, there the marks remained, like the blotting-paper of his crime. Casts of them were taken at once, and carefully have they been stored by me.

The shoemaker, a shrewd but talkative man, said unasked that he had never seen such boots as had left those marks, since the "Young Squire" (he meant Mr. Edgar Vaughan) went upon his travels. For this gratuitous statement, he was strongly rebuked by the coroner.

For the rest, all that could be found out, after close inquiry, was, that a stranger darkly clad had been seen by the gamekeepers, in a copse some half-mile from the house, while the men were beating for woodcocks on the previous day. He did not seem to be following my father, and they thought he had wandered out of the forest road. He glided quickly away, before they could see his features, but they knew that he was tall and swarthy. No footprints were found in that ride like those by the shrubbery spring.

I need not say what verdict the coroner's jury found.

CHAPTER III.

THUS far, I have written in sore haste, to tell, as plainly and as briefly as possible, that which has darkened all my life. Though it never leaves my waking thoughts, to dwell upon it before others is agony to me. Henceforth my tale will flow perhaps more easily, until I fall again into a grief almost as dark, and am struck by storms of passion which childhood's stature does not reach.

When the shock of the household, and the wonder of the county, and the hopes of constables (raised by a thousand pounds' reward) had subsided gradually, my mother continued to live in the old mansion, perhaps because none of her friends came forward to remove her. Under my father's will she was the sole executrix; but all the estates (including house and park) were left to my father's nearest relative, as trustee for myself, with a large annuity to my mother charged upon them.

There were many other provisions and powers in the will, which are of no consequence to my story. The chief estate was large and rich, extending three or four miles from the house, which stood in a beautiful part of Gloucestershire. The entire rental was about 12,000*l.* a year. My father (whose name was Henry Valentine Vaughan), being a very active man in the prime of life, had employed no steward, but managed everything himself. The park, and two or three hundred acres round it, had always been kept in hand; the rest was let to thriving tenants, who loved (as they expressed it) "every hair on the head of a Vaughan." There was also a small farm near the sea, in a lonely part of Devonshire; but this was my mother's, having been left to her by her father, a clergyman in that neighbourhood.

My father's nearest relative was his half-brother, Edgar Vaughan, who had been educated for the Bar, and at one time seemed likely to become eminent; then suddenly he gave up his practice, and resided (or rather roved) abroad, during several years. Sinister rumours about him reached our neighbourhood, not long before my father's death. To these, however, the latter paid no attention, but always treated his brother Edgar with much cordiality and affection. But all admitted that Edgar Vaughan had far outrun his income as a younger son, which amounted to about 600*l.* a year. Of course, therefore, my father had often helped him.

On the third day after that night, my guardian came to Vaughan Park. He was said to have hurried from London, upon learning there what had happened.

The servants and others had vainly and foolishly tried to keep from me the nature of my loss. Soon I found out all they knew, and when the first fit and horror left me, I passed my whole time, light or dark, in roving from passage to passage, from room to room, from closet to closet, searching every chink and cranny for the murderer of my father. Though heretofore a timid child, while so engaged I knew not such a thing as fear; but peered, and groped, and listened, feeling every inch of wall and wainscot, crawling lest I should alarm my prey, spying through the slit of every door, and shaking every empty garment. Certain boards there were near the east window which sounded hollow; at these I scooped·until I broke my nails. In vain nurse Maples locked me in her room, held me at her side, or even bound me to the bed. My ravings forced her soon to yield, and I would not allow her, or any one else, to follow me. The Gloucester physician said that since the disease of my mind had taken that shape, it would be more dangerous to thwart than to indulge it.

It was the evening of the third day, and weary with but never *of* my search, I was groping down the great oak-staircase in the dusk, hand after hand, and foot by foot, when suddenly the main door-bell rang. The snow was falling heavily, and had deadened the sound of wheels. At once I slid (as my father had taught me to do) down the broad balustrade, ran across the entrance-hall, and with my whole strength drew back the bolt of the lock. There I stood in the porch, un-frightened, but with a new kind of excitement on me. A tall dark man came up the steps, and shook the snow from his boots. The carriage-lamp shone in my face. I would not let him cross the threshold, but stood there and confronted him. He pretented to take me for some servant's child, and handed me a parcel covered with snow. I flung it down, and said, looking him full in the face, "I am Clara Vaughan, and you are the man who killed my father." "Carry her in, John," he said to the servant—"carry her in, or the poor little thing

will die. What eyes !" and he used some foreign oath—
" what wonderful eyes she has !"

That burst of passion was the last conscious act of
the young and over-laboured brain. For three months
I wandered outside the gates of sorrow. My guardian,
as they told me, was most attentive throughout the
whole course of the fever, and even in the press of business visited me three times every day. Meanwhile,
my mother was slowly shaking off the stupor which lay
upon her, and the new fear of losing me came through
that thick heaviness, like the wind through a fog.
Doubtless it helped to restore her senses, and awoke
her to the work of life. Then, as time went on, her
former beauty and gentleness came back, and her reason
too, as regarded other subjects. But as to that which
all so longed to know, not a spark of evidence could be
had from her. The faintest allusion to that crime, the
name of her loved husband, the mere word "murder"
uttered in her presence—and the consciousness would
leave her eyes, like a loan withdrawn. Upright she sat
and rigid as when she was found that night, with the
lines of her face as calm and cold as moonlight. Only
two means there were by which her senses could be

restored : one was low sweet music, the other profound sleep. She was never thrown into this cataleptic state by her own thoughts or words, nor even by those of others when in strict sequence upon her own. But any attempt to lead her to that one subject, no matter how craftily veiled, was sure to end in this. The skilful physician, who had known her many years, judged, after special study of this disease, in which he felt deep interest, that it was always present in her brain, but waited for external aid to master her. I need not say that she was now unfit for any stranger's converse, and even her most careful friends must touch sometimes the motive string.

As I recovered slowly from long illness, the loss of my best friend and the search for my worst enemy revived and reigned within me. Sometimes my guardian would deign to reason with me upon what he called "my monomania." When he did so, I would fix my eyes upon him, but never tried to answer. Now and then, those eyes seemed to cause him some uneasiness ; at other times he would laugh and compare them pleasantly to the blue fire-damp in a coal-mine. His dislike of their scrutiny was well known to me, and incited me the more to urge it. But in spite of all, he was ever kind and gentle to me, and even tried some grimly playful overtures to my love, which fled from him with loathing, albeit a slow conviction formed that I had wronged him by suspicion.

Edgar Malins Vaughan, then about thirty-seven years old, was (I suppose) a very handsome man, and perhaps of a more striking presence than my dearest father. His face, when he was pleased, reminded me strongly of the glance and smile I had lost, but never could it convey that soft sweet look, which still came through the clouds to me, now and then in dreams. The outlines of my guardian's face were keener too and stronger, and his complexion far more swarthy. His eyes were of a hard steel-blue, and never seemed to change. A slight lameness, perceptible only at times, did not impair his activity, but served him as a pretext for declining all field-sports, for which (unlike my father) he had no real taste.

His enjoyments, if he had any—and I suppose all men have some—seemed to consist in the management of the estate (which he took entirely upon himself), in satiric literature and the news of the day, or in lonely rides and sails upon the lake. It was hinted too, by Thomas Henwood, who disliked and feared him strangely, that he drank spirits or foreign cordials in his own room, late at night. There was nothing to confirm this charge; he was always up betimes, his hand was never tremulous, nor did his colour change.

CHAPTER IV.

My life—childhood I can scarcely call it—went quietly for several years. The eastern wing of the house was left unused, and rarely traversed by any but myself. Foolish tales, of course, were told about it; but my frequent visits found nothing to confirm them. At night, whenever I could slip from the care of good but matter-of-fact Ann Maples, I used to wander down the long corridor, and squeeze through the iron gate now set there, half in hope and half in fear of meeting my father's spirit. For such an occasion all my questions were prepared, and all the answers canvassed. My infant mind was struggling ever to pierce the mystery which so vaguely led its life. Years only quickened my resolve to be the due avenger, and hardened the set resolve into a fatalist's conviction. My mother, always full of religious feeling, taught me daily in the Scriptures, and tried to make me pray. But I could not take the mild teachings of the Gospel as a little child. To me the Psalms of David, and those books of the Old Testament which recount and seem to applaud revenge, were sweeter than all the balm of Gilead; they supplied a terse and vigorous form to my perpetual yearnings. With a child's impiety, I claimed for myself the mission of the Jews against the enemies of the Lord. The forms of prayer, which my mother taught me, I mumbled through, while looking in her gentle face, with anything but a prayerful gaze. For my own bedside I kept a widely different form, which even now I shudder to repeat. And yet I loved dear mother truly, and pitied her sometimes with tears; but the shadow-love was far the deeper.

My father's grave was in the churchyard of the little village which clustered and nestled beyond our lodge. It was a real grave. The thought of lying in a vault had always been loathsome to him, and he said that it struck him cold. So fond was he of air and light and freedom, the change of seasons and weather, and the shifting of the sun and stars, that he used to pray that they still might pass over his buried head; that he might lie, not in the dark lockers of death, but in the open hand of time. His friends used to think it strange that a man of so light and festive nature should ever talk of death; yet so he often did, not morbidly, but with good cheer. In pursuance, therefore, of his well-known wish, the vaults wherein there lay five centuries of Vaughan dust were not opened for him; neither was his grave built over with a hideous ash-bin; but lay narrow, fair, and humble, with a plain, low headstone of the whitest marble, bearing his initials deeply carved in grey. Through our warm love and pity, and that of all the village, and not in mere compliance with an old usage of the western counties, his simple bed was ever green and white with the fairest of low flowers. Though otherwise too moody and reckless to be a gardener, I loved to rear from seed his favourite plants, and keep them in my room until they blossomed; then I would set them carefully along his grave, and lie down beside it, and wonder whether his spirit took pleasure in them.

But more often, it must be owned, I laid a darker tribute there. The gloomy channel into which my young mind had been forced was overhung, as might be expected, by a sombre growth. The legends of midnight spirits, and the tales of blackest crime, shed their poison on me. From the dust of the library I exhumed all records of the most famous atrocities, and devoured them at my father's grave. As yet I was too young to know what grief it would cause to him who slept there, could he but learn what his only child was doing. That knowledge would at once have checked me, for his presence was ever with me, and his memory cast my thoughts, as moonlight shapes the shadows.

The view from the churchyard was a lovely English scene. What higher praise can I give than this? Long time a wanderer in foreign parts, nothing have I seen that comes from nature to the heart like a true English landscape.

The little church stood back on a quiet hill, which bent its wings in a gentle curve to shelter it from the north and east. These bending wings were feathered, soft as down, with larches, hawthorn, and the lightly-pencilled birch, between which, here and there, the bluff rocks stood their ground. Southward, and beyond the glen, how fair a spread of waving country we could see! To the left, our pretty lake, all clear and calm, gave back the survey of the trees, until a bold gnoll, fringed with alders, led it out of sight. Far away upon the right, the Severn stole along its silver road, leaving many a reach and bend, which caught towards eventide the notice of the travelled sun. Upon the horizon might be seen at times, the blue distance of the Brecon hills.

Often when I sat here all alone, and the evening dusk came on, although I held those volumes on my lap, I could not but forget the murders and the revenge of men, the motives, form, and evidence of crime, and nurse a vague desire to dream my life away.

Sometimes also my mother would come here, to read her favourite Gospel of St. John. Then I would lay the dark records on the turf, and sit with my injury hot upon me, wondering at her peaceful face. While, for her sake, I rejoiced to see the tears of comfort and contentment dawning in her eyes, I never grieved that the soft chastenment was not shed on me. For her I loved and admired it; for myself I scorned it utterly.

The same clear sunshine was.upon us both: we both were looking on the same fair scene—the gold of ripening corn, the emerald of woods and pastures, the crystal of the lake and stream; above us both the peaceful heaven was shed, and the late distress was but a night gone by—wherefore had it left to one the dew of life, to the other a thunderbolt? I knew not the reason then, but now I know it well.

Although my favourite style of literature was not likely to improve the mind, or yield that honeyed melancholy which some young ladies woo, to me it did but little harm. My will was so bent upon one object, and the whole substance and shape of my thoughts so stanch in their sole ductility thereto, that other things went idly by me, if they showed no power to promote my end. But upon palpable life, and the doings of nature I became observant beyond my age. Things in growth or motion round me impressed themselves on my senses, as if a nerve were touched. The uncoiling of a fern-frond, the shrinking of a bind-weed blossom, the escape of a cap-pinched bud, the projection of a seed, or the sparks from a fading tuberose, in short, the lighter prints of Nature's sandalied foot, were traced and counted by me. Not that I derived a maiden pleasure from them, as happy persons do, but that it seemed my business narrowly to heed them.

As for the proud phenomena of imperial man, so far as they yet survive the crucible of convention—the lines where cunning crouches, the smile that is but a brain-flash, the veil let down across the wide mouth of greed, the guilt they try to make volatile in charity,— all these I was not old and poor enough to learn. Yet I marked unconsciously the traits of individuals, the mannerism, the gesture, and the mode of speech, the complex motive, and the underflow of thought. So all I did, and all I dreamed, had one colour and one aim.

My education, it is just to say, was neglected by no one but myself. My father's love of air and heaven had descended to me, and nothing but my mother's prayers or my own dark quest could keep me in the house. Abstract principles and skeleton dogmas I could never grasp ; but whatever was vivid and shrewd and native, whatever had point and purpose, was seized by me and made my own. My faculties were not large, but steadfast now, and concentrated.

Though several masters tried their best, and my governess did all she could, I chose to learn but little. Drawing and music (to soothe my mother) were my principal studies. Of poetry I took no heed, except in the fierce old drama.

Enough of this. I have said so much, not for my sake, but for my story.

CHAPTER V.

On the fifth anniversary of my father's death, when I was fifteen years of age, I went to visit (as I always did upon that day) the fatal room. Although this chamber had been so long unused, the furniture was allowed to remain ; and I insisted passionately that it should be my charge. What had seemed the petulance of a child was now the strong will of a thoughtful girl.

I took the key from my bosom, where I always kept it, and turned it in the lock. No mortal had entered that door since I passed it in my last paroxysm, three weeks and a day before. I saw a cobweb reaching from the black finger-plate to the third mould of the beading. The weather had been damp, and the door stuck fast to the jamb, then yielded with a crack. Though I was bold that day, and in a mood of triumph, some awe fell on me as I entered. There hung the heavy curtain, last drawn by the murderer's hand; there lay the bed-clothes, raised for the blow, and replaced on death ; and there was the pillow where sleep had been so prolonged. All these I saw with a forced and fearful glance, and my breath stood still as the wind in a grave.

Presently a light cloud floated off the sun, and a white glare from the snow of the morning burst across the room. My sight was not so dimmed with tears as it generally was when I stood there, for I had just read the history of a long-hidden crime detected, and my eyes were full of fierce hope. But stricken soon to the wonted depth of sadness, with the throbs of my heart falling like the avenger's step, I went minutely through my death-inspection. I felt all round the dusty wainscot, opened the wardrobes and cupboards, raised the lids of the deep-bayed window-seats, peered shuddering down the dark closet, where I believed the assassin had lurked, started and stared at myself in the mirror, to see how lone and wan I looked, and then approached the bed, to finish my search in the usual place, by lying and sobbing where my father died. I had glanced beneath it and round the pillars, and clutched the curtain as if to squeeze out the truth, and was just about to

throw myself on the coverlet and indulge the fit so
bitterly held at bay, when something on the hangings
above the head-board stopped me suddenly. There I
saw a narrow line of deep and glowing red. It grew so
vivid on the faded damask, and in the white glare of the
level sun, that I thought it was on fire. Hastily setting
a chair by the pillar, for I would not tread on that bed,
I leaped up, and closely examined the crimson vein.

Without thinking, I knew what it was—the heart-
blood of my father. There were three distinct and
several marks, traced by the reeking dagger. The first
on the left, which had caught my glance, was the broadest
and clearest to read. Two lines, meeting at a right
angle, rudely formed a Roman L. Rudely I say, for
the poniard had been too rich in red ink, which had
clotted where the two strokes met. The second letter
was a Roman D, formed also by two bold strokes, the
upright very distinct, the curve less easily traced at the
top, but the lower part deep and clear. The third letter
was not so plain. It looked like C at first, but upon
further examination I felt convinced that it was meant
for an O, left incomplete through the want of more
writing fluid ; or was it then that my mother had seized

the dark author by the hair, as he stooped to incline his
pen that the last drop might trickle down?

Deciphering thus with fingers and eyes, I traced these
letters of blood, one by one, over and over again, till
they danced in my gaze like the northern lights. I
stood upon tiptoe and kissed them; I cared not what I
was doing: it was my own father's blood, and I thought
of the heart it came from, not of the hand which shed it.
When I turned away, the surprise, for which till then I
had found no time, broke full upon me. How could
these letters, in spite of all my vigilance, so long have
remained unseen? Why did the murderer peril his life
yet more by staying to write the record, and seal perhaps the conviction of his deed? And what did these
characters mean? Of these three questions, the first was
readily solved. The other two remained to me as new
shadows of wonder. Several causes had conspired to
defer so long this discovery. In the first place, the
damask had been of rich lilac, shot with a pile of car-
mine, which, in the waving play of light, glossed at once
and obscured the crimson stain, until the fading hues of
art left in strong contrast nature's abiding paint.
Secondly, my rapid growth and the clearness of my eyes

that day lessened the distance and favoured perception.
Again—and this was perhaps the paramount cause—the
winter sun, with rays unabsorbed by the snow, threw
his sheer dint upon that very spot, keen, level, and un-
coloured—a thing which could happen on few days in the
year, and for few minutes each day, and which never
had happened during my previous search. Perhaps
there was also some chemical action of the rays of light
which evoked as well as showed the colour ; but of this
I do not know enough to speak. Suffice it that the
letters were there, at first a great shock and terror, but
soon a strong encouragement to me.

My course was at once to perpetuate the marks and
speculate upon them at leisure, for I knew not how
fleeting they might be.   I hurried downstairs, and
speaking to no one procured some clear tissue paper.
Applying this to the damask, and holding a card behind,
I carefully traced with a pencil so much of the letters
as could be perceived through the medium, and com-
pleted the sketch by copying most carefully the rest.
It was, however, beyond my power to keep my hand
from trembling. A shade flitted over my drawing—oh,
how my heart leaped !

When I had finished the pencil-sketch, and before it was inked over (for I could not bring myself to paint it red), I knelt where my father died and thanked God for this guidance to me. By the time I had dried my eyes the sun was passed and the lines of blood were gone, even though I knew where to seek them, having left a pin in the damask. By measuring I found that the letters were just three feet and a quarter above the spot where my father's head had been. The largest of them, the L, was three inches long and an eighth of an inch in width; the others were nearly as long, but nothing like so wide.

Trembling now, for the rush of passion which stills the body was past, and stepping silently on the long silent floor, I went to the deep dark-mullioned window and tried to look forth. After all my lone tumult, perhaps I wanted to see the world. But my jaded eyes and brain showed only the same three letters burning on the snow and sky. Evening, a winter evening, was fluttering down. The sun was spent and stopped by a grey mist, and the landscape full of dreariness and cold. For miles, the earth lay white and wan, with nothing to part life from death. No step was on the snow, no wind among the trees; fences, shrubs, and hillocks were as wrinkles in a winding-sheet, and every stark branch had like me its own cold load to carry.

. But on the left, just in sight from the gable-window, was a spot, black as midnight, in the billowy snow. It was the spring which had stored for me the footprints. Perhaps I was superstitious then; the omen was accepted. Suddenly a last gleam from the dauntless sun came through the ancient glass, and flung a crimson spot upon my breast. It was the red heart, centre of our shield, won with Cœur de Lion.

Oh scutcheons, blazonments, and other gewgaws, by which men think to ennoble daylight murders, how long shall fools account it honour to be tattooed with you? Mercy, fellow-feeling, truth, humility, virtues that never flap their wings, but shrink lest they should know they stoop, what have these won? Gaze sinister, and their crest a pillory.

With that red pride upon my breast, and that black heart within, and my young form stately with revenge, I was a true descendant of Crusaders.

CHAPTER VI.

To no one, not even to Thomas Henwood (in whom I confided most), did I impart the discovery just described. Again and again I went to examine those letters, jealous at once of my secret, and fearful lest they should vanish. But though they remained perhaps unaltered, they never appeared so vivid as on that day.

With keener interest I began once more to track, from page to page, from volume to volume, the chronicled steps of limping but sure-footed justice.

Not long after this I was provided with a companion. "Clara," said my guardian one day at breakfast, "you live too much alone. Have you any friends in the neighbourhood?"

"None in the world, except my mother."

"Well, I must try to survive the exclusion. I have done my best. But your mother has succeeded in finding a colleague. There's a cousin of yours coming here very soon."

"Mother dear," I cried in some surprise, "you never told me that you had any nieces."

"Neither have I, my darling," she replied, "nor any nephews either; but your uncle has; and I hope you will like your visitor."

"Now remember, Clara," resumed my guardian, "it is no wish of mine that you should do so. To me it is a matter of perfect indifference; but your mother and myself agreed that a little society would do you good."

"When is she to come?" I asked, in high displeasure that no one had consulted me.

"He is likely to be here to-morrow."

"Oh," I exclaimed, "the plot is to humanize me through a young gentleman, is it? And how long is he to stay in my house?"

"In *your* house! I suppose that will depend upon your mother's wishes."

"More likely upon yours," I cried; "but it matters little to me."

He said nothing, but looked displeased; my mother doing the same, I was silent, and the subject dropped. But of course I saw that he wished me to like his new

importation, while he dissembled the wish from knowledge of my character.

Two years after my father's birth, his father had
married again. Of the second wedlock the only offspring
was my guardian, Edgar Vaughan. He was a posthu-
mous son, and his mother in turn contracted a second
marriage. Her new husband was one Stephen Daldy,
a merchant of some wealth. By him she left one son,
named Lawrence, and several daughters. This Lawrence
Daldy, my guardian's half-brother, proved a spendthrift,
and, while scattering the old merchant's treasure married
a fashionable adventuress. As might be expected, no
retrenchment ensued, and he died in poverty, leaving an
only child.

This boy, Clement Daldy, was of my own age, or
thereabout, and, in pursuance of my guardian's plan,
was to live henceforth with us.

He arrived under the wing of his mother, and his
character consisted in the absence of any. If he had any
quality at all by which one could know him from a doll,
it was perhaps vanity; and if his vanity was singular
enough to have any foundation, it could be only in his
good looks. He was, I believe, as pretty a youth as ever

talked without mind, or smiled without meaning. Need it be said that I despised him at once unfathomably?

His mother was of a very different order. Long-enduring, astute, and plausible, with truth no more than the pith of a straw, she added thereto an imperious spirit, embodied just now in an odious meekness. Whatever she said or did, in her large contempt of the world, her lady-abbess walk, and the chastened droop of her brilliant eyes, she conveyed through it all the impression of her humble superiority. Though profoundly convinced that all is vanity, she was reluctant to force this conviction on minds of a narrower scope, and dissembled with conscious grace her knowledge of human nature.

To a blunt, outspoken child, what could be more disgusting? But when upon this was assumed an air of deep pity for my ignorance, and interest in my littleness, it became no longer bearable.

This Christian Jezebel nearly succeeded in estranging my mother from me. The latter felt all that kindness towards her which people of true religion, when over-charitable, conceive towards all who hoist and salute the holy flag. Our sweet pirate knew well how to make the most of this.

For myself, though I felt that a hypocrite is below the level of hate, I could not keep my composure when with affectionate blandness our visitor dared to "discharge her sacred duty of impressing on me the guilt of harbouring thoughts of revenge." Of course, she did not attempt it in the presence of my mother; but my guardian was there, and doubtless knew her intention.

It was on a Sunday after the service, and she had stayed for the sacrament.

"My sweet child." she began, "you will excuse what I am about to say, as I only speak for your good, and from a humble sense that it is the path of duty. It has pleased God, in His infinite wisdom, to afflict your dear mother with a melancholy so sensitive, that she cannot bear any allusion to your deeply-lamented father. You have therefore no female guidance upon a subject which justly occupies so much of your thoughts. Your uncle Edgar, in his true affection for you, has thought it right that you should associate more with persons calculated to develop your mind."

Now I hate that word "develop;" and I felt my passion rising, but let her go on :—

"Under these circumstances, it grieves me deeply, my poor dear child, to find you still display a perversity, and a wilful neglect of the blessed means of grace, which must (humanly speaking) draw down a judgment upon you. Now, open your heart to me, the whole of your little unregenerate heart, you mysterious but (I firmly believe) not ill-disposed lambkin. Tell me all your thoughts, your broodings, your dreams—in fact, your entire experiences. Uncle Edgar will leave the room, if you wish it."

"Certainly not," I said.

"Quite right, my dear; have no secrets from one who has been your second father. Now tell me all your little troubles. Make me your mother-confessor. I take the deepest interest in you. True, I am only a weak and sinful woman, but my chastisements have worked together for my edification, and God has been graciously pleased to grant me peace of mind."

"You don't look as if you had much," I cried.

Her large eyes flashed a quick start from their depths, like the stir of a newly-fathomed sea. My guardian's face gleamed with a smile of sly amusement. Recovering at once her calm objective superiority, she proceeded :

"I have been troubled and chastened severely, but now I perceive that it was all for the best. But perhaps it is not very graceful to remind me of that. Yet, since all my trials have worked together for my good, on that account I am, under Providence, better qualified to advise you, in your dark and perilous state. I have seen much of what thoughtless people call 'life.' But in helping you, I wish to proceed on higher principles than those of the world. You possess, beyond question, a strong and resolute will, but in your present benighted course it can lead only to misery. Now, what is the principal aim of your life, my love ?"

"The death of my father's murderer."

"Exactly so. My unhappy child, I knew it too well. Though a dark sin is your leading star, I feel too painfully my own shortcomings, and old unregenerate tendencies, to refuse you my carnal sympathy. You know my feelings, Edgar."

"Indeed, Eleanor," replied my guardian, with an impenetrable smile, "how should I ? You have always been such a model of every virtue."

She gave him a glance, and again addressed me. "Now suppose, Clara Vaughan, that, after years of brooding and lonely anguish, you obtain your revenge at last, who will be any the better for it ?"

"My father and I."

"Your father indeed! How you wrong his sweet and most forgiving nature !"

This was the first thing she had said that touched me ; and that because I had often thought of it before. But I would not let her see it.

"Though his nature were an angel's," I cried, "as I believe it was, never could he forgive that being who tore him from me and my mother. I know that he watches me now, and must be cold and a wanderer, until I have done my duty to him and myself."

"You awful child. Why, you'll frighten us all. But you make it the more my duty. Come with me now, and let me inculcate the doctrines of a higher and holier style."

"Thank you, Mrs. Daldy, I want no teaching, except my mother's."

"You are too wilful and headstrong for her. Come to me, my poor stray lamb."

" I would sooner go to a butcher, Mrs. Daldy."

" Is it possible? Are you so lost to all sense of right?"

"Yes, if you are right," I replied; and left the room.

Thenceforth she pursued tactics of another kind. She tried me with flattery and fictitious confidence, likely from a woman of her maturity to win a young girl, by inflating self-esteem: she even feigned a warm interest in my search, and wished to partake in my readings and secret musings. Indeed, I could seldom escape her. I am ready to own that, by her suggestions and quick apprehension, she gained some ascendancy over me, but not a tenth part of what she thought she had won ; and I still continued to long for her departure. Of this, however, no symptom appeared: she made herself quite at home, and did her best to become indispensable to my mother.

Clement Daldy had full opportunity to commend himself to my favour. We were constantly thrown together, in the presence of his mother, and the absence of mine. For a long time, I was too young, and too much engrossed by the object for which I lived, to have any inkling of their scheme; but suddenly a

suspicion broke upon me. My guardian and his sister-
in-law had formed, as I thought, a deliberate plot for
marrying me, when old enough, to that tailor's block.
The one had been so long accustomed to the lordship of
the property, to some county influence, and great
command of money, that it was not likely he would
forego the whole without a struggle. But he knew
quite well that the moment I should be of age I would
dispense with his wardship, and even with his residence
there, and devote all I had to the pursuit of my
"monomania." All his endeavours to make me his
thrall had failed, partly from my suspicions, partly from
a repugnance which could not be conquered. Of course,
I intended to give him an ample return for his
stewardship, which · had been wise and unwearying.
But this was not what he wanted. The motives of his
accomplice require no explanation. If once this neat
little scheme should succeed, I must remain in their
hands, Clement being nobody, until they should happen
to quarrel for me.

To show what Clement Daldy was, a brief anecdote
is enough. When we were about sixteen years old, we
sat in the park one morning, at the corner of the lake;

Clement's little curled spaniel, which he loved as much as he could love anything, was gambolling round us. As the boy lounged along, half asleep, on the rustic chair, with his silky face shaded by a broad hat, and his bright curls glistening like daffodils playing, I thought what a pretty peep-show he made, and wondered whether he could anyhow be the owner of a soul.

"Oh, Clara," he lisped, as he chanced to look up—"Couthin Clara, I wish you wouldn't look at me tho."

"And did it look fierce at its dolly?" I said; for I was always good-natured to him. "Dolly knows I wouldn't hurt it, for it's house full of sugar-plums."

"Then do let me go to thleep; you are such a howwid girl."

So I hushed him off with a cradle song. But before the long lashes sunk flat on his cheeks, like the ermine tips on my muff, and while his red lips yet trembled like cherries in the wind, my attention was suddenly drawn to the lake. There was a plashing, and barking, and hissing, and flapping of snow-white wings—poor Juan engaged in unequal combat with two fierce swans who had a nest on the island. The poor little dog, though he fought most gallantly, was soon driven into deep water, and the swans kept knocking him under with rapid and powerful strokes. Seeing him almost drowned, I called Clement to save him at once.

" I can't," said the brave youth; " you go if you like. They'll kill me, and I can't bear it; and the water ith tho cold."

In a moment I pushed off the boat which was near, jumped into it, and, seizing an oar, contrived to beat back the swans, and lifted the poor little dog on board, gasping, half-drowned, and woefully beaten. Meanwhile my lord elect had leaped on the seat for safety, and was wringing his white little hands, and dancing and crying, " Oh, Clara'll be throwned, and they'll say it was me. Oh, what thall I do! what thall I do!"

Even when I brought him his little pet safe, he would not touch him, because he was wet; so I laid him full on his lap.

CHAPTER VII.

THE spring of the year 1849 was remarkable, throughout the western counties, for long drought. I know
not how it may be in the east of England, but I have
observed that in the west long droughts occur only in
the spring and early summer. In the autumn we have
sometimes as much as six weeks without rain, and in
the summer a month at most, but all the real droughts
(so far as my experience goes) commence in February
or March; these are, however, so rare, and April has
won such poetic fame for showers, and July for heat
and dryness, that what I state is at variance with the
popular impression.

Be that as it may, about Valentine's-day, 1849, and
after a length of very changeable weather, the wind
fixed its home in the east, and the sky for a week
was grey and monotonous. Brilliant weather ensued;
white frost at night, and strong sun by day. The frost

became less biting as the year went on, and the sun more powerful; there were two or three overcast days, and people hoped for rain. But no rain fell, except one poor drizzle, more like dew than rain.

With habits now so ingrained as to become true pleasures, I marked the effects of the drought on all the scene around me. The meadows took the colour of Russian leather, the cornlands that of a knife-board. The young leaves of the wood hung pinched and crisp, unable to shake off their tunics, and more like catkins than leaves. The pools went low and dark and thick with a coppery scum (in autumn it would have been green), and little bubbles came up and popped where the earth cracked round the sides. The tap-rooted plants looked comely and brave in the morning, after their drink of dew, but flagged and flopped in the afternoon, as a clubbed cabbage does. As for those which had only the surface to suck, they dried by the acre, and powdered away like the base of a bonfire.

The ground was hard as horn, and fissured in stars, and angles, and jagged gaping cracks, like a dissecting map or a badly-plastered wall. It amused me sometimes to see a beetle suddenly cut off from his home by that which to him was an earthquake. How he would run to and fro, look doubtfully into the dark abyss, then, rising to the occasion, bridge his road with a straw. The snails shrunk close in their shells, and resigned themselves to a spongy distance of slime. The birds might be seen in the morning, hopping over the hollows of the shrunken ponds, prying for worms, which had shut themselves up like caddises deep in the thirsty ground. Our lake, which was very deep at the lower end, became a refuge for all the widgeons and coots and moorhens of the neighbourhood, and the quick-diving grebe, and even the summer snipe, with his wild and lonely "cheep." The brink of the water was feathered, and dabbled with countless impressions of feet of all sorts—dibbers, and waders, and wagtails, and weasels, and otters, and foxes, and the bores of a thousand bills, and muscles laid high and dry.

For my own pet robins I used to fill pans with water along the edge of the grass, for I knew their dislike of the mineral spring (which never went dry), and to these they would fly down and drink, and perk up their impudent heads, and sluice their poor little dusty wings; and then, as they could not sing now, they would give me a chirp of gratitude.

When the drought had lasted about three months, the east wind, which till then had been cold and creeping, became suddenly parching hot. Arid and heavy, and choking, it panted along the glades, like a dog on a dusty road. It came down the water-meadows, where the crowsfoot grew, and wild celery, and it licked up the dregs of the stream, and powdered the flood-gates, all skeletons now, with grey dust. It came through the copse, and the young leaves shrunk before it, like a child from the hiss of a snake. The blast pushed the doors of our house, and its dry wrinkled hand was laid on the walls and the staircase and woodwork; a hot grime tracked its steps, and a taint fell on all that was fresh. As it folded its baleful wings, and lay down like a desert dragon, vegetation, so long a time sick, gave way at last to despair, and flagged off flabbed and dead. The clammy grey dust, like hot sand thrown from ramparts, ate to the core of every-thing, choking the shrivelled pores and stifling the languid breath. Old gaffers were talking of murrain in cattle, and famine and plague among men, and farmers were too badly off to grumble.

But the change even now was at hand. The sky which had long presented a hard and cloudless blue, but trailing a light haze round its rim in the morning, was bedimmed more every day with a white scudding vapour across it. The sun grew larger and paler, and leaned more on the heavens, which soon became ribbed with white skeleton-clouds; and these in their turn grew softer and deeper, then furry and ravelled and wisped. One night the hot east wind dropped, and, next morning (though the vane had not changed), the clouds drove heavily from the south-west. But these signs of rain grew for several days before a single drop fell; as is always the case after discontinuance, it was hard to begin again. Indeed, the sky was amassed with black clouds, and the dust went swirling like a mat beaten over the trees, and the air became cold, and the wind moaned three days and three nights, and yet no rain fell. As old Whitehead, the man at the lodge, well observed, it had "forgotten the way to rain." Then it suddenly cleared one morning (the 28th of May), and the west was streaked with red clouds, that came up to crow at the sun, and the wind for the time was lulled, and the hills looked close to my hand. So I went to my father's grave without the little green watering-pot or a trowel to fill the chinks, for I knew it would rain that very day.

In the eastern shrubbery there was a pond, which my father had taken much trouble to make and adorn; it was not fed by the mineral spring, for that was thought likely to injure the fish, but by a larger and purer stream, called the "Witches' brook," which, however, was now quite dry. This pond had been planted around and through with silver-weed, thrumwort and sun-dew, water-lilies, arrow-head, and the rare double frog-bit, and other aquatic plants, some of them brought from a long distance. At one end there was a grotto, cased with fantastic porous stone, and inside it a small fountain played. But now the fountain was silent, and the pond shrunk almost to its centre. The silver eels which once had abounded here, finding their element likely to fail, made a migration, one dewy night, overland to the lake below. The fish, in vain envy of that great enterprise, huddled together in the small wet space which remained, with their back-fins here and there above water. When any one came near, they dashed away, as I have seen grey mullet do in the shallow sea-side pools. Several times I had water poured in for their benefit, but it was gone again directly. The mud round the edge of the remnant puddle was baked and cracked, and foul with an oozy green sludge, the relic of water-weeds.

This little lake, once so clear and pretty, and full of bright dimples and crystal shadows, now looked so forlorn and wasted and old, like a bright eye worn dim with years, and the trees stood round it so faded and wan, the poplar unkempt of its silver and green, the willow without wherewithal to weep, and the sprays of the birch laid dead at its feet; altogether it looked so empty and sad and piteous, that I had been deeply grieved for the sake of him who had loved it.

So, when the sky clouded up again, in the afternoon of that day, I hastened thither to mark the first effects of the rain.

As I reached the white shell-walk, which loosely girt the pond, the lead-coloured sky took a greyer and woollier cast, and overhead became blurred and pulpy; while round the horizon it lifted in frayed festoons.

As I took my seat in the grotto, the big drops began to patter among the dry leaves, and the globules rolled in the dust, like parched peas. A long hissing sound ensued, and a cloud of powder went up, and the trees moved their boughs with a heavy dull sway. Then broke from the laurels the song of the long-silent thrush, and reptiles, and insects, and all that could move, darted forth to rejoice in the freshness. The earth sent forth that smell of sweet newness, the breath of young nature awaking, which reminds us of milk, and of clover, of balm, and the smile of a child.

But, most of all, it was in and around the pool that the signs of new life were stirring. As the circles began to jostle, and the bubbles sailed closer together, the water, the slime, and the banks, danced, flickered, and darkened, with a whirl of living creatures. The surface was brushed, as green corn is flawed by the wind, with the quivering dip of swallows' wings; and the ripples that raced to the land splashed over the feet of the wagtails.

Here, as I marked all narrowly, and seemed to rejoice in their gladness, a sudden new wonder befell me. I was watching a monster frog emerge from his penthouse of ooze, and lift with some pride his brown spots and his bright golden throat from the matted green cake of dry weed, when a quick gleam shot through the fibres. With a listless curiosity, wondering whether the frog, like his cousin the toad, were a jeweller, I advanced to the brim of the pool. The poor frog looked timidly at me with his large starting eyes; then, shouldering off the green coil, made one rapid spring, and was safe in the water. But his movement had further disclosed some glittering object below. Determined to know what it was, despite the rain, I placed some large pebbles for steps, ran lightly, and lifted the weed. Before me lay, as bright as if polished that day, with the jewelled hilt towards me, a long narrow dagger. With a haste too rapid for thought to keep up, I snatched it, and rushed to the grotto.

There, in the drought of my long revenge, with eyes on fire, and teeth set hard and dry, and every root of my heart cleaving and crying to heaven for blood, I pored on that weapon, whose last sheath had been— how well I knew what. I did not lift it towards God, nor fall on my knees and make a theatrical vow; for that there was no necessity. But for the moment my life and my soul seemed to pass along that cold blade, just as my father's had done. A treacherous, blue, three-cornered blade, with a point as keen as a viper's fang, sublustrous like ice in the moonlight, sleuth as hate, and tenacious as death. To my curdled and fury-struck vision it seemed to writhe in the gleam of the storm which played along it like a corpse-candle. I fancied how it had quivered and rung to find itself deep in that heart.

My passions at length overpowered me, and I lay, how long I know not, utterly insensible. When I came to myself again, the storm had passed over, the calm pool covered my stepping stones, the shrubs and trees wept joy in the moonlight, the nightingales sang in the elms, healing and beauty were in the air, peace and content walked abroad on the earth. The May moon slept on the water before me, and streamed through the grotto arch; but there it fell cold and ghost-like upon the tool of murder. Over this I hastily flung my scarf; coward, perhaps I was, for I could not handle it then, but fled to the house and dreamed in my lonely bed.

When I examined the dagger next day, I found it

to be of foreign fabric. "Ferrati, Bologna," the name and abode of the maker, as I supposed, was damascened on the hilt. A cross, like that on the footprint, but smaller, and made of gold, was inlaid on the blade, just above the handle. The hilt itself was wreathed with a snake of green enamel, having garnet eyes. From the fine temper of the metal, or some annealing process, it showed not a stain of rust, and the blood which remained after writing the letters before described had probably been washed off by the water. I laid it most carefully by, along with my other relics, in a box which I always kept locked.

So God, as I thought, by His sun, and His seasons, and weather, and the mind He had so prepared, was holding the clue for me, and shaking it clear from time to time, along my dark and many-winding path.

CHAPTER VIII.

Soon after this, a ridiculous thing occurred, the con-
sequences of which were grave enough. The summer
and autumn after that weary drought were rather wet
and stormy. One night towards the end of October, it
blew a heavy gale after torrents of rain. Going to the
churchyard next day, I found, as I had expected, that
the flowers so carefully kept through the summer were
shattered and strewn by the tempest; and so I returned
to the garden for others to plant in their stead. My
cousin Clement (as he was told to call himself) came
sauntering towards me among the beds. His usual
look of shallow brightness and empty self-esteem had
failed him for the moment, and he looked like a fan-
tailed pigeon who has tumbled down the horse-rack.
He followed me to and fro, with a sort of stuttering
walk, as I chose the plants I liked best; but I took

little notice of him, for such had been my course since I first discovered their scheme.

At last, as I stooped to dig up a white verbena, he came behind me, and began his errand with more than his usual lisp. This I shall not copy, as it is not worth the trouble.

" Oh, Clara," he said, " I want to tell you something, if you'll only be good-natured ! "

" Don't you see I am busy now ? " I replied, without turning to look. " Won't it do when you have taken your curl-papers off ? "

" Now, Clara, you know that I never use curl-papers. My hair doesn't want it. You know it's much prettier than your long waving black stuff, and it curls of its own accord, if mamma only brushes it. But I want to tell you something particular."

" Well, then, be quick, for I am going away." And with that I stood up and confronted him. He was scarcely so tall as myself, and his light showy dress and pink rose of a face, which seemed made to be worn in the hair, were thrown into brighter relief by my sombre apparel and earnest twilight look. Some lurking sense of this contrast seemed to add to his hesitation. At last he began again :

"You know, Cousin Clara, you must not be angry with me, because it isn't my fault."

"What is not your fault?"

"Why, that I should fall—what do they call it?—fall in love, I suppose."

"You fall in love, you dissolute doll! How dare you fall in love, sir, without my leave?"

"Well, I was afraid to ask you, Clara. I couldn't tell what you would say."

"Oh, that must depend, of course, on who Mrs. Doll is to be! If it's a good little thing with blue satin arms, and a sash and a slip, and pretty blue eyes that go with a string, perhaps I'll forgive you, poor child, and set you up with a house, and a tea-set, and a mother-of-pearl perambulator."

"Now, don't talk nonsense," he answered. "Before long I shall be a man, and then you'll be afraid of me, and put up your hands, and shriek, and want me to kiss you."

I had indulged him too much, and his tongue was taking liberties. I soon stopped him.

"How dare you bark at me, you wretched little white-woolled nursery dog?"

I left him, and went with my basket of flowers along the path to the churchyard. For a while he stood there frightened, till his mother looked forth from the drawing-room window. Between the two fears he chose the less, and followed me to my father's grave. I stood there and angrily waved him back, but he still persisted, though trembling.

"Cousin Clara," he said—and his lisp was quite gone, and he tried to be in a passion—"Cousin Clara, you *shall* hear what I have got to say. You have lived with me now a long time, and I'm sure we have agreed very well, and I—I—no, I don't see why we should not be married."

"Don't you indeed, sir?"

"Perhaps," he continued, "you are afraid that I don't care about you. Really now, I often think that you would be very good-looking, if you would only laugh now and then, and leave off those nasty black gowns; and then if you would only leave off being so grand, and mysterious, and stately, and getting up so early, I would let you do as you liked, and you might paint me and have a lock of my hair."

"Clement Daldy," I asked, "do you see that lake?"

"Yes," he replied, turning pale, and inclined to fly.

"There's water enough there now. If you ever dare again to say one word like this to me, or even to show by your looks that you think it, I'll take you and drown you there, as sure as my father lies here."

He slunk away quickly without a word, and could eat no lunch that day. In the afternoon, as I sat in my favourite bow-window seat, Mrs. Daldy glided in. She had put on with care her clinging smile, as she would an Indian shawl. I thought how much better her face would have looked with its natural, bold, haughty gaze.

"My dear Clara," began this pious tidewaiter, "what have you done to vex so your poor cousin Clement?"

"Only this, Mrs. Daldy: he was foolish or mad, and I gave him advice in a truly Christian spirit, entirely for his own good."

"I hope, my dear, that some day it may be his duty as well as his privilege to advise you. But, of course, you need not take his advice. My Clara loves her own way as much as any girl I ever knew; and with poor Clement she will be safe to have it."

"No doubt of that," I replied.

"And then, my pet, you will be in a far better position than you could attain as an unmarried girl to pursue the great aim of your life ; so far, I mean, as is not inconsistent with the spirit of Christian forgiveness. Your guardian has thought of that, in effecting this arrangement ; and I trust that I was not wrong in allowing so fair a prospect, under Providence, of your ultimate peace of mind to influence me considerably when he sought my consent."

"I am sure I am much obliged to you."

"I cannot conceal from you, so clear-sighted as you are—and if I could, I object to concealment of any kind, on principle—that there are also certain worldly advantages, which are not without weight, however the heart be weaned by trials and chastened from transient things. And your guardian has this arrangement so very much at heart. My own dear child, I have felt for you so long that I love you as a daughter. How thankful I ought to be to the Giver of all good things to have you really my own dear child."

"Be thankful, madam, when you have got it. This is a good thing which under Providence you must learn to do without.

It was coarse of me to hint at my riches. But what could I do with her ?

"Why, Clara," she asked, in great amazement, "you cannot be so foolish and wilful as to throw away this chance of revenge? If only for your dear mother's sake, as well as your father's, it is the path of duty. Let me tell you, both she and yourself are very much more in your guardian's power than you have any idea. And what would be your poor father's wish, who has left you so entirely to his brother's care and discretion? Will you put off for ever the discovery of his murderer?"

"My father," I said, proudly, "would scorn me for doing a thing below him and myself. The last of the Vaughans to be plotted away to a grocer's doll!"

It had been a trial of temper; and contempt was too much for hypocrisy. Through the rouge of the world, and the pearl-powder of religion, nature flushed forth on her cheek; for she really loved her son. She knew where to wound me the deepest.

"Is it no condescension in us that my beautiful boy should stoop to the maniac-child of a man who was stabbed—stabbed in his midnight bed—to atone, no doubt, for some low act of his own?"

I sprang up, and rang the bell. Thomas Henwood,

who made a point of attending me, came at once. I
said to him, calmly and slowly:

"Allow this person one hour to pack her things.
Get a fly from the Walnut Tree Inn, and see her
beyond the Lodge."

If I had told him to drag her away by the hair, I
believe that man would have done it. She shrunk away
from me; for the moment her spirit was quelled, and
she trembled into a chair.

"I assure you, Clara, I did not mean what I said.
You provoked me so."

"Not one word more. Leave the room and the house."

"Miss Vaughan, I will not leave this house until
your guardian returns."

"Thomas," I said, without looking towards her, "if
Mrs. Daldy is not gone in an hour, you quit my service."

How Thomas Henwood managed it, I never asked.
He was a resolute man, and all the servants obeyed him.
She turned round once, as she crossed the threshold, and
gave me a look which I shall never forget. Was such
the look that had glared on my father before the blow?
She lifted the white arm of which she was proud, and
threw back her head, like the Fecial hurling his dart.

"Clara Vaughan, you shall bitterly grieve for this. It shall throw you and your mother at the feet of your father's murderer, and you shall crave meat worse than your enemy's blood."

Until she had quitted the house, I could not sit down; but went to my father's bedroom, where I often took refuge when strongly excited and unable to fly to his grave. The thoughts and the memories hovering and sighing around that fatal chamber were enough to calm and allay the sensations of trivial wrong.

But now this was not the case. The outrage offered had been, not to me, but to him who seemed present there. The suggestion, too, of an injury done by my father, though scorned at first, was working and ruffling within me, as children put bearded corn-ears in another's sleeve, which by-and-by work their own way to the breast. Till now, I had always believed that some worldly advantage or gain had impelled my foe to the deed which left me an orphan. But that woman's dark words had started a new train of reasoning, whose very first motion was doubt of the man I worshipped. Among all I had ever met, there existed but one opinion as to what he had been—a true gentleman, who had injured not one of God's creatures, whose life had been guided mainly by the wishes and welfare of others. Moreover, I had my own clear recollections—his voice, his eyes, and his smile, his manner and whole expression; these, it is true, were but outward things, yet a child's intuition is strong and hard to refute.

Again, during my remembrance, he had never been absent from us, except for a day or two, now and then, among his county neighbours; and any ill will which he might have incurred from them must, from his position, have become notorious.

And yet, in the teeth of this reasoning, and in spite of my own warm feeling, that horrible suspicion clave to my heart and chilled it like the black spot of mildew. And what if the charge were true? In that case, how was I better than he who had always been to my mind a fiend in special commission? His was vengeance, and mine revenge; he had suffered perhaps a wanton wrong, as deep to his honour as mine to my love.

While I was brooding thus miserably, my eyes fell upon the bed. There were the red streaks, grained and fibred like the cross-cut of a fern-stalk; framed and looking down on me, the sampler of my life. Drawing near, I trembled with an unknown awe, to find myself in that lonely presence, not indeed thinking, but inkling such things of my father, my own darling father, whose blood was looking at me. In a storm of self-loathing and sorrow, I knelt there and sobbed my atonement; but never thenceforth could I wholly bar out the idea. Foul ideas when once admitted will ever return on their track, as the cholera walks in the trail of its former pall.

But instead of abating my dogged pursuit, I now had a new incentive—to dispel the aspersions cast on my father's shadow.

CHAPTER IX.

AT this particular time of my life, many things began to puzzle me, but nothing was a greater puzzle than the character of my guardian. Morose or moody he was not, though a stranger might have thought him so; nor could I end with the conviction that his heart was cold. It rather seemed to me as if he felt that it ought to be so, and tried his best to settle down as the inmate of an icehouse. But any casual flush of love, any glow of native warmth from the hearts around him, and taken by surprise he wavered for one traitor moment, and in his eyes gleamed some remembrance, like firelight upon frozen windows. But let any one attempt to approach him then with softness, to stir kind interest and feeling into benevolent expression, and Mr. Vaughan would promptly shut himself in again, with a bar of irony, or a bolt of sarcasm. Only to my mother was his behaviour different; towards her his manner was so gentle, and his tone so kind, that but for my conviction that remorse lay under it, I must have come to like him. True, they did not often meet, for dear mother confined herself (in spite of Mrs. Daldy) more and more closely to her own part of the house, and rarely had the spirits now to share in the meals of the family. Therefore, I began at once to take her place, and would not listen to Mrs. Daldy's kind offer to relieve me. This had led quite recently to a little outbreak. One day I had been rather late for dinner, and, entering the room with a proud apology, found to my amazement Mrs. Daldy at the head of the table. For me a seat was placed, as for a good little girl, by the side of Master Clement. At first I had not the presence of mind to speak, but stood by my rival's chair, waiting for her to rise. She affected not to understand me, and began, with her hand on the ladle, and looking me full in the face: "I fear, darling Clara, the soup is cold; but your uncle can give you a very nice slice of salmon. Have you offered thanks for these mercies?"

"Thank you, I will take soup. Allow me to help myself. I am sorry to have troubled you."

And I placed my hand on the back of her chair, presuming that she would get up ; but she never stirred one inch, and actually called for a plate to help me. My guardian was looking at both of us, with a dry smile of amusement, and Clement began to simper and play with his fork.—Now for it, or never, thought I. "Mrs. Daldy, you quite mistake me, or pretend to do so. Have the goodness to quit *my* chair."

She had presumed on my dread of an altercation before the servants, but only Thomas Henwood happened to be in the room. Had there been a dozen present, I would still have asserted my right. At last she rose in her stateliest manner, but with an awkward smile, and a still more awkward sneer.

"Your use, my poor child, of the possessive pronoun is far more emphatic than your good breeding is."

"Who cares for your opinion ?" Not a hospitable inquiry ; but then she was not *my* visitor.

In grand style she marched to the door, but soon thought better of it, and came to her proper place with the sigh of a contrite spirit.

"Poor creature ! It is a rebuke to me, for my want of true faith in the efficacy of prayer."

And after all this, she made a most excellent dinner.

About that woman there was something of a slimy pride, no more like to upright prickly self-respect than macerated bird-lime is to the stiff bright holly. Yet no one I ever knew possessed such wiry powers of irritation. Whenever my mother and my guardian met, she took care to be in the way, and watched them both, and appealed to me with all her odious pantomime of sorrow, sympathy, wonder, loving superiority, and spiritual yearnings. And all the time her noisome smile, like the smell of a snake, came over us. She knew, and rejoiced in the knowledge, how hard set I was to endure it, and every quick flash of my eyes only lit up her unctuous glory.

For all I know, it was natural that my antipathy to that woman should, by reaction, thaw sometimes my coldness towards my uncle. Though self-respect had at length compelled him to abandon his overtures to my friendship, now and then I detected him looking at me with a pitying regard. In self-defence, I began to pity him, and ceased to make faces or sneer when the maids —those romantic beings—declared that he must have been crossed in love. At this conclusion, long ago, all the servants' hall had arrived; and even little Tilly

Jenkins, not admitted as yet to that high conclave, remarkable only for living in dust-bins, and too dirty to cause uneasiness to the under-shoeboy's mother—even that Tilly, I say, ran up to me one morning (when I went to see my dear pony) and beat out her dust, and then whispered:

"Oh, please, Miss Clara, to give my very best wishes to Master. What a terrible blight to the heart be unrequited love!" And Tilly sighed a great cloud of brick-dust.

"Terrible, Tilly: I hope you have not fallen in love with the weeding boy!"—a smart young lad, ten stairs at least above her.

"Me, miss? Do you think I would so demean myself?" And Tilly caught up her dust-pan arrogantly.

This little anecdote proves a fact which I never could explain, viz. that none of the servants were ever afraid of me.

To return to the straight line of history. My guardian came home rather late that evening, and some hours after the hasty exit of Mrs. and Master Daldy. While I was waiting in some uneasiness, it struck me that he had kept out of the way on purpose, lest he should seem too anxious about the plot. Mrs. Daldy, as I found afterwards, had written to him from the inn, describing my "frenzied violence, and foaming Satanic fury"— perhaps I turned pale, no more—and announcing her intention to remain at Malvern, until she should be apprised whether uncle or niece were the master. In the latter case she demanded—not that she cared for mammon, but as a humble means for the advancement of the Kingdom—the sum of 300*l.*; that being the lowest salary conscience allowed her to specify for treading the furnace of affliction, to save the lost sheep of the house of Israel. I forgot to say that, before she left the house, she had tried to obtain an interview with my mother, hoping, no doubt, to leave her in the cataleptic state. But this had been sternly prevented by Thomas Henwood, who performed quite a labour of love in ministering the expulsion. All the servants hated her as a canting sneak and a spy.

That night when I received Mr. Edgar Vaughan's short missive—" Clara, I wish to see you immediately in my study," my heart began to flutter provokingly,

and the long speech I had prepared flew away in shreds
of rhetoric. Not that I meant for an instant to bate
one tittle of what I had done and would do: but I
had never asserted my rights as yet in direct opposition
to him, nor taken upon my own shoulders the guar-
dianship of myself. But the dreary years of dark
preparation and silent welding of character had
braced a sensitive, nervous nature with some little
self-reliance.

With all the indifference I could muster, I entered
the gloomy room, and found him leaning upon the high
desk where he kept the accounts of his stewardship.
The position was chosen well. It served at once to
remind me of his official relation, and to appeal to
the feelings as betokening an onerous wardship. Of
late his health had been failing him, and after every
long absence from home, he returned more jaded and
melancholy. Now a few silver hairs—no more than a
wife would have quickly pulled out—were glistening
among his black locks; but though he was weary
and lonesome, he seemed to want none to love him,
and his face wore the wonted sarcastic and travelled
look.

As our glances met, we both saw that the issue was joined which should settle for life the mastery. He began in a light and jocund manner, as if I were quite a small thing.

"Well done, Miss Clara, you *are* asserting yourself. Why, you have dismissed our visitors with very scant ceremony."

"To be sure I have; and will again, if they dare to come back."

"And don't you think that you might have consulted your mother or me?"

"Most likely I should have done so, in an ordinary case."

"Then your guardian was meant for small matters! But what was the wonder to-day?"

"No wonder at all. Mrs. Daldy insulted my father, and I sent her out of his house."

"What made her insult my brother?"

"My refusal to marry her puppet and puppy."

"Clement Daldy! Did she propose such a thing? She must think very highly of you!"

"Then I think very lowly."

"And you declined, did you, Clara?"

"No. I refused."

"Very good. No one shall force you; there is plenty of time to consider the subject."

"One moment is too much."

"Clara, I have long noticed in you a rude, disrespectful, and I will say (in spite of your birth) a low and vulgar manner towards me, your uncle and guardian. Once for all, I will not permit it, child."

"*Child* you call me, do you? Me, who am just seventeen, and have lived seven such years as I have, and no one else!"

He answered quite calmly, and looking coldly at me:

"I never argue with women. Much less with girls. Mrs. Daldy comes back to-morrow. You will beg her pardon, as becomes a young lady who has forgotten herself. The other question may wait."

"I thought, sir, that you had travelled far, and in many countries."

The abrupt inquiry startled him, and his thoughts seemed to follow the memory.

"What if I have?" he asked, at length, and with a painful effort.

"Have you always found women do just what you chose?"

He seemed not to listen to me; as if he were out of hearing: then laughed because I was looking at him.

"Clara," he said, "you are an odd girl, and a Vaughan all over. I would rather be your friend than your enemy. If you cannot like me, at least forget your dislike of me, and remember that I am your uncle, and have tried to make you love me."

"And what if I do not?"

"Then I must keep you awhile from the management of this property. My dear brother would have wished it, until you recover your senses; and not an acre of it is legally yours."

This he said so slowly, and distinctly, and entirely without menace, that, knowing his manner, I saw it was the truth, at least in his opinion. Strange as it may seem, I began at once to revolve, not the results of dispossession and poverty on myself, or even on my mother, but the influence which the knowledge of this new fact must have on my old suspicions, surmises, and belief.

"Will the property pass to you?" I asked.

"Yes, if I choose: or at any rate the bulk of it."

"What part will be yours? Do you mean to say the house?—"

"Never mind now. I would rather leave things as they are, if you will only be more sensible."

"I will not disguise my opinions for a hundred Vaughan Parks, or a thousand Vaughan Palaces; no, nor even to be near my father's bones."

"Very well," he said, "just as you like. But for your mother's sake, I give you till Christmas to consider."

"If you bring back Mrs. Daldy, I shall leave the door as she enters it."

"I have no wish to hurry you," he replied, "and therefore she shall not return at present. Now take these papers with you. You may lay them before any lawyer you please. They are only copies, but may be compared with the originals, which I have. They will quickly prove how totally you are at my discretion."

"The money and the land may be so, but not I. Before I go, answer me one question. Did you know of these things, whatever they may be, before my father's death?"

He looked at me clearly and calmly, with no withdrawal, or conscious depth in his eyes, and answered:

" No.   As a gentleman, I did not."

I felt myself more at a loss than ever, and for the moment could not think.

CHAPTER X.

THUS was I, and, what mattered much more, my mother, reduced quite suddenly from a position of rank and luxury, and a prospective income of £15,000 a-year (so much had the land increased in value) to a revenue of nothing, and no home. Even to me it was a heavy blow, but what could my poor mother do?

We were assured by counsel that a legal struggle could end in expense alone, and advised by the family lawyers to throw ourselves on the good feeling and appeal to the honour of Mr. Edgar Vaughan. Mr. Vaughan he must henceforth be called. I cannot well understand, still less can I explain, small and threadbare technicalities (motes, which too often are the beam of Justice), but the circumstances which robbed me of my father's home were somewhat as follows :—

By the will of my father's grandfather, Hubert Vaughan, who died in the year 1782, the whole of the family property was devised to his son, Vaughan Powis Vaughan, for life, and after his decease, to his sons successively *in tail male*, failing these to his right heirs in general. This will was said to have been prepared in haste: it was, in fact, drawn by a country attorney, when the testator was rapidly sinking. It was very brief, and by no means accurately worded; neither did it contain those powers to meet family exigencies, which I am told a proper practitioner would have inserted.

There was no reason to suppose that the testator had contemplated anything more than a strict settlement of the usual kind, *i.e.* a common estate entail, expectant upon a life-interest; and under which I should have succeeded my father, as his heiress, in the ordinary course. But it is the chief fault of smatterers in the law (and country attorneys at that time were no better) that they will attempt to be too definite. The country lawyer in this case, grossly ignorant of his profession, and caught by the jangle of the words *tail male*, had inserted them at hazard, possibly not without some idea that they would insure a stricter succession than a common entail would do.

When my father became of age, measures were taken for barring the entail created by the will of Hubert Vaughan; and at the time it was believed that these were quite effectual, and therefore that my father was now entitled in fee-simple, and could dispose of the property.

Upon his marriage with my mother, she, with worthy pride, refused most firmly to accept a jointure charged on his estates, alleging that as she brought no fortune into the family, she would not incumber the family property, which had but recently been relieved of incumbrances. More than this—she had even insisted upon expressly abandoning, by her marriage settlement, all claim to dower. This unusual course she had adopted, because of some discontent expressed by relatives of my father at his marriage with a portionless bride, whereby her self-respect had been deeply wounded. So nothing was settled upon her, except her own little estate in Devonshire, which was secured to her separate use.

My father had never permitted this excess of generosity on her part, but that he was by nature careless upon such subjects, and hoped to provide amply for her interests by his will: moreover he was hot to remove all obstacles to their marriage. But it was now discovered that he had no power to charge the real estate for her benefit, in the manner his will imported; that he had never been more than a tenant in tail, and that entail such that I could not inherit. Neither, of course, could I take under his will, as he possessed no power of disposition. One quarter of all that has been written upon the subject I never could understand; and even as to the simplest points, sometimes I seem to apprehend them clearly, and then I feel that I do not. My account of the matter is compressed from what I remember of the legal opinions.

The leading fact, at any rate, and the key to all the mischief, was, that the entail had never been barred at all: the legal process (called a " recovery ") which was to have had that effect, being null and void through some absurd informality. They told me something about a tenant to a precipice, but they must have made a mistake, for there was no precipice on the estate, unless some cliffs near the church could be called so, and they were never let.

Be that as it may, my father's will was declared to be waste paper, except as regarded what they called the personalty, or, in good English, the money he had to bequeath. And of this there was very little, for, shortly before his death, he had spent large sums in drainage, farm-buildings, and other improvements. Furthermore, he had always maintained a profuse hospitality, and his charity was most lavish. The lawyers told us that, under the circumstances (a favourite expression of theirs when they mean some big robbery), a court of equity would perhaps consider our application to be "recupped," as they called it, out of the estate, for the money laid out in improvements under a false impression. But we had been cupped enough already. Grossly plundered by legal jargon, robbed by statute, and scourged by scriveners' traditions, we flung away in disgust the lint the bandits offered, and left them "all estate, right, title, interest, and claim, whether at law or in equity, in to or out of" the licking of our blood.

But now my long suspicions, and never-discarded conviction of my guardian's guilt, were, by summary process, not only revived, but redoubled. This arose partly from the discovery of the stake he had on my father's life, and partly, perhaps, from a feeling of hatred towards our supplanter. That he knew not till now the flaw in our title, and his own superior claim, was more than I could believe. I felt sure that he had gained this knowledge while in needy circumstances and sharp legal practice, brought, as he then most probably was, into frequent contact with the London agents who had the custody of the documents.

To be in the same room with him, was now more than I could bear, and it became impossible that we should live any longer in the same house. He, indeed, wished, or feigned to wish, that we should remain there, and even showed some reluctance to urge his un- righteous rights. But neither my mother (who bore the shock with strange resignation) nor myself would hear of any compromise, or take a farthing at his hands, and he was too proud and stern to press upon us his compunctions.

Statements of our case had been prepared and sub- mitted to three most eminent conveyancers, and the three opinions had been found to agree, except upon some trivial points. More than two months had been thus consumed, and it was now once more the anni- versary of my father's death. I had spent the time in narrowly watching my ex-guardian's conduct, though keeping aloof, as much as possible, from any intercourse with him.

One night, I stole into the room which he called his study, and where (with a child's simplicity) I believed him to keep his private documents. Through Thomas Henwood, to whom I now confided almost everything, and whose suspicions were even stronger than mine, I obtained clandestine possession of the keys of the large bureau. As I stood before that massive repository in the dead of night, the struggle within me was intense and long. What letters, what journals, documents, or momentous relics of a thousand kinds, might be lurking here, waiting only for a daughter's hand to turn the lock, and cast the light she bore on the death-warrant of her father! How easy then to snatch away the proof, clutching it, though it should burn the hand or bosom, to wave it, with a triumph wilfully prolonged, before the eyes of justice's dull-visioned ministers; and then to see, without a shudder or a thrill of joy, but with the whole soul gazing, the slow, struggling, ghastly expiation. As this thought came crawling through my heart, lighting up its depth as would a snake of fire, the buhl before

me grew streaks of blood, and the heavy crossbars a
gallows.　I lifted my hand to open the outer lock.
Already the old cruciform key was trembling in the
silver scutcheon.　I raised the lamp in my left hand
to show the lunette guard which curved above the hole,
when a heavy mass all cold and dark fell across my
eyes.　I started, and thought for the moment, in my
strong excitement, that it was my father's hand.　One
instant more, and, through the trembling of my senses,
I saw that it was only a thick fold of my long black
hair, shaken down on the face by my bending and
quivering posture.　But the check was enough.　A
Vaughan, and that the last one of so proud and frank
a race, to be prowling meanly, with a stolen tool, to
violate confidence, and pry through letters!　No suspicion, however strong, nothing short of certainty (if
even that) could warrant it.　Driven away by shame
combined with superstition, I glided from the cold
silent room, and restored the keys to my faithful
friend, whom I had left in the passage, ordering
him at once to replace them, and never touch them
again.

　"Well, miss," he whispered, with a smile, "I knew

you couldn't do it, because I seemed, somehow, it wasn't like a Vaughan."

We were already preparing to quit the house, no longer ours, when our dismissal became abrupt, through another act of mine. What drove me to such a wild deed I can scarcely tell. Shame, perhaps, for the furtive nature of my last attempt hurried me into the other extreme; and now I was so shaken by conflicting impulse, that nothing was too mad for me.

On the seventh anniversary of my father's death, and the last which I was likely ever to spend beneath that roof, I passed the whole day in alternate sadness and passion, in the bedroom where he died. All the relics I possessed, both of his love and of his death, I brought thither; and spread them out, and wept upon the one, and prayed upon the other. I also brought my choicest histories of murder and revenge, and pored over them by the waning daylight and the dull lamp, and so on through the night, until my mind became the soul's jetsam.

Then I procured four very large wax candles, and lit them at the head of the bed, two on each side, and spread a long white cloth between, as if my father were lying in state ; and hung a row of shorter lights above, to illuminate the letters of blood. Then I took a small alarum clock, given me by dear father, that I might rise for early walks with him, and set it upon a chest by the door, and fixed it so as to ring five minutes before the hour at which the murder befell. A cold presentiment crawled through me that, at the fatal time, I should see the assassin. After all these arrangements I took my volume again, and sat in the shade of the curtain, with a strong light on the page. I was deep in some horrible record, and creeping with terror and hope, when the clear bell rang a long and startling peal. I leaped up, like one shot through the heart, and what I did was without design or purpose. My glance fell on the dagger; I caught it up, and snatched the lamp, and hurried down corridor and staircase, straight to my guardian's private room.

He was sitting at the table, for he never passed that night in bed. At the sound of the lock he leaped up, and pointed a pistol, then hid it. Straight up to him I went, as swiftly and quietly as a spirit, and spoke :

"Seven years ago, at this very moment, my father was killed. Do you know this dagger ?" He started back, as if I had stabbed him with it, then covered his eyes with both hands.

"You know it, then?" I said, with a triumph chill all over me. "It was your hand that used it."

Another moment, and I should have struck him with it. I lifted it in my frenzy; when he looked at me by some wonderful effort, calmly, steadily, even coldly. "Yes," he said, "I have seen that weapon before. Alas my poor dear brother!"

Whether it was true feeling that made his voice so low and deep, or only fierce self-control, I knew not then, nor tried to think.

"You know who owned it?" I asked, with my life upon his answer.

"Yes. I know who owned it once; but many years ago. And I know not in the least what is become of him now."

The baffled fury and prostrate hope—for at the moment I fully believed him—were too much for my reeling brain and fasting body. For one minute's command of my faculties, I would have sold them for ever; but I felt them ebbing from me, as the life does from a wound. The hemispheres of my brain were parting one from the other, and a grey void spreading between them. I tried to think, but could not. I strove to say *anything*, but failed. Fainter and fainter grew the room, the lamp, the ceiling, the face at which I tried to look. Things went to and fro with a quicker quiver, like flame in the wind, then, round and round like whirling water; my mouth grew stiff, and the tongue between my teeth felt like a glove; and with a rush of sound in my brain and throat, and a scream pent up, yet bursting, I fell, as I thought, through the earth. I was only on the floor, in a fit.

When I came to myself, I was in my own bed, and my own dear mother bending over me, pale, and haggard, and full of tears. The broad daylight was around us, and the faint sunshine on her face. She had been with me ever since. In my weakness, I looked up at her with a pang of self-reproach, to think how little I had valued her love; and I vowed to myself to make up for it by future care and devotion.

That violent convulsion, and the illness after it, changed me not a little both in mind and body.

CHAPTER XI.

IT was indeed high time for me to cherish my mother
Her pain at leaving the place where she had known
her little all of happiness—for her childhood had been
overcast with trouble—her pain was so acute and over-
powering that all my deep impassioned feelings sunk
reproved before it.

My guardian now seemed much embittered against
me, and anxious for our departure. He came once or
twice, in my illness, to ask for and to see me; and he
brought back, unperceived by any one, the weapon for
which I raved. But ere I was quite recovered, he
wrote, requesting to see me on business in his study.
I could not speak yet without pain, having bitten my
tongue severely.

" Your mother shall have a home here," he said, " as
long as ever she wants one; but as for you, malignant
or mad, I will try no more to soften you. When first I

saw you in your early childhood, you flew at me as a
murderer.   Soon after you ransacked my cupboards and
stole my boots, to compare them with some impressions
or casts you kept.   Yes, you look astonished.   I never
told you of it, but I knew it for all that.   Of those
absurdities I thought little, for I regarded them as the
follies of a mad child, and I pitied you deeply, and even
liked you for your filial devotion.   But now I find that
you have grown up in the same belief, and you dare
even now to avow it.   You know that I have no fear of
you."

"Then why had you got that pistol?"

I saw that he was vexed and surprised at my having
perceived it.

"In a house like this, where such deeds have been
done, I think it right to be armed.   Do you think if I
had feared you, or your evidence, I would have restored
that dagger?"

"Whose was it?"

"I told you the other night that I once saw a weapon
like it, for which at first I mistook it, but closer examination convinced me of the difference."

"How does it differ?"

"In this. There was no snake on the handle of the other, though there was the cross on the blade."

"And where did you see the other?"

"Some day I will tell you. It is not right to do so now."

"Not convenient to you, I suppose you mean."

"I have also shown you that the lock of hair found in your poor mother's hand is much finer and more silky than mine; and you know that I cannot draw on my foot a boot so small as the one whose impression you have. But I am ashamed of myself for having stooped to such proofs as these. Dare you to look at me and suppose that I with my own hand could have stabbed my brother, a brother so kind and good to me, and for whose sake alone I have borne so long with you?"

He tried to look me down. I have met but one whose gaze could master mine; and he was not that one.

"So, you doubt me still? Are your things packed?'

"Yes, and my mother's."

"Then if your mother is well enough, and will not let you leave her, you had better go next week."

"No," I replied, "we will go to-morrow."

"Wilful to the last. So be it. Take this; you cannot refuse it in duty to your mother."

He put in my hand an order for a large sum of money.
I threw it into the fire.

"There have been criminals," I exclaimed, "who have
suffered from a life-long fear, lest the widow and
orphans, starved through their crime, should compass
their dying bed. Though we starve in a garret, we
touch no bread of yours."

"Bravo, Miss Melodrame. You need never starve in
the present state of the stage."

"That I don't understand; but this I do. It is perhaps the last time I shall ever see you living. Whether
you did that deed or not is known to God, and you, and
possibly one other. But whether you did it or not, I
know it is on your soul. Your days are wretched, your
nights are troubled. You shall die as your brother died,
but not so prepared for death."

"Good bye, Clara. My lunch is coming up."

God has much to forgive me, but nothing worse than
the dark thought of that speech. In my fury at weakness in such a cause, I had dared sometimes to imagine
that my mother knew him to be the murderer, but con-
cealed it for the sake of the family honour!

CHAPTER XII.

No need to recount my bitter farewell to all the scenes and objects I had loved so long, to all which possessed a dark yet tender interest, and most of all to my father's grave. That some attention might still be paid to this, I entrusted it to the care of an old housekeeper of ours, who was living in the village. My last visit was in the moonlight, and dear mother was there. I carried rather than led her away. Slight as my knowledge has been of lightsome and happy love, I am sure that a sombre affection is far the stronger and sweeter.

As we began our journey, a crowd of the villagers met us beyond the lodge, and lined the Gloucester road as far as the old oak-tree. While our hired conveyance passed between them, the men stood mute with their hats in their hands, the women sobbed and curtseyed, and blessed us, and held up their children to look at us.

Our refuge was the small estate or farm in Devonshire, which I have mentioned as my mother's property.

This, which produced £45 a-year, was all that now remained to us, except a sum of £1,000 left to me by a
godfather, and of which I could not touch the principal.
The residue of the personalty, and the balance at the
banker's, we had refused to take, being assured that legally
we were responsible to Mr. Vaughan, even for the back
rents of the Gloucestershire estate. Of course we had
plenty of jewellery, some of it rather valuable, but the
part most precious was heirloom, and that we had left
behind. Most of our own had been my father's gift, and
therefore we could not bear to sell it.

As regarded myself, this comparative poverty was not
of very great moment, except as impairing my means of
search ; but for my mother's sake I was cut to the heart,
and lost in perplexity. She had so long been accustomed
to much attention and many luxuries, which her weak
health had made indispensable to her. Thomas Henwood and poor Ann Maples insisted on following our
fortunes, at one third of their previous wages. My
mother thought it beyond our means to keep them even
so ; but for her sake I resolved to try. I need not say
that I carried all my relics, difficult as it was to hide
them from my mother.

When we reached our new home, late in the evening of the second day, a full sense of our privation for the first time broke upon us. It was mid-winter, and in the gloom of a foggy night, and after the weariness of a long journey, our impressions were truly dismal. Jolted endlessly up and down by ruts a foot deep and slaty stones the size of coal-scuttles, entombed alive betwixt grisly hedges which met above us like the wings of night, then obliged to walk up treadmill hills while the rickety fly crawled up behind; then again plunging and lurching down some corkscrew steep to the perpetual wood and rushing stream at the bottom; at length and at last along a lane so narrow that it scraped us on both sides as we passed, a lane which zig-zagged every thirty yards with a tree-bole jutting at every corner, at length and at last we came to the farmyard gate. It was not far from the lonely village of Trentisoe, which lies some six miles to the west of Lynmouth. This part is little known to London tourists, though it possesses scenery of a rarer kind than Lynmouth itself can show.

Passing through an outer court, with a saw-pit on one side and what they call a " linhay " on the other, and where a slop of straw and " muck " quelched under the wheels, we came next to the farmyard proper, and so (as the flyman expressed it) "home to ouze." The "ouze" was a low straggling cottage, jag-thatched, and heavy-eaved, and reminded me strongly of ragged wet horse-cloths on a rack. The farmer was not come home from Ilfracombe market, but his wife, Mrs. Honor Huxtable, soon appeared in the porch, with a bucket in one hand and a candle stuck in a turnip in the other. In the cross-lights, we saw a stout short woman, brisk and comely, with an amazing cap, and cheeks like the apples which they call in Devonshire "hoary mornings."

"A massy on us, Zuke," she called into the house, "if here bain't the genelvolks coom, and us be arl of a muck! Hurn, cheel, hurn for thee laife to the calves' ouze, and toorn out both the pegs, and take the pick to the strah, and gie un a veed o' wets."

Having thus provided for our horse, she advanced to us.

"So, ye be coom at last! I be crule glad to zee e, zure enough. Baint e starved amost! An unkid place it be for the laikes of you."

So saying, she hurried us into the house, and set us before a wood-fire all glowing upon the ground, beneath

an enormous chimney podded with great pots and crocks
hung on things like saws. These pots, like Devonshire
hospitality, were always boiling and chirping. The
kitchen was low, and floored with lime and sand, which
was worn into pits such as boys use for marbles; but
the great feature was the ceiling. This was divided by
deep rafters into four compartments lengthwise. Across
some of these, battens of wood were nailed, forming a
series of racks, wherein reposed at least a stye-ful of
bacon. Herbs and stores of many kinds, and ropes of
onions dangled between.

Mrs. Huxtable went to the dresser, and got a large
dish, and then turned round to have a good look at us.

"Poor leddy," she said gently, "I sim her's turble
weist and low. But look e zee, there be a plenty of
bakken yanner, and us'll cut a peg's drort to-morrow, and
Varmer Badcock 'll zend we a ship, by rason ourn be
all a'lambing." Then she turned to me.

"Whai, Miss, you looks crule unkid tu. Do e love
zider?"

"No, Mrs. Huxtable. Not very much. I would
rather have water."

"Oh drat that wash, e shan't have none of thiccy.

Us has got a brown gearge of beer, and more nor a dizzen pans of mulk and crame."

Her chattering warmth soon put us at our ease; and as soon as the parlour fire burnt up, she showed us with many apologies, and "hopping no offence" the room which was thenceforth to be ours.

After tea, I put my dear mother to bed as soon as possible, and sat by the dying fire to muse upon our prospects. Not the strangeness of the place, the new ideas around me, not even my weariness after railroad, coach, and chaise, could keep my mind from its one subject. In fact, its colour had now become its form.

To others indeed, all hope of ever detecting and bringing to justice the man, for whose death I lived, might seem to grow fainter and fainter. Expelled from that place, and banished from those recollections, where, and by which alone, I could well expect ever to wind up my clue, robbed of all means of moving indifferent persons and retaining strong ones; and, more than this, engrossed (as I must henceforth be) in keeping debt at bay, and shielding my mother from care—what prospect was there, nay what possibility, that I a weak unaided girl, led only by set will and fatalism, should ever overtake and grasp a man of craft, and power, and desperation?

It mattered not: let other things be doubtful, unlikely, or impossible; let the hands of men be clenched against me, and the ears of heaven be stopped; let the earth be spread with thick darkness, as the waters are spread with earth, and the murderer set Sahara between us, or turn hermit on the Andes; happen what would, so God were still above us, and the world beneath our feet—I was as sure that I should send that man from the one to the throne of the other, as he was sure to be dragged away thence, to fire, and chains, and gnashing of teeth.

CHAPTER XIII.

So impulsive, kind-hearted, and honest was Mrs. Huxtable, that we could always tell what was the next thing she was going to say or do. Even at her meals she contrived to be in a bustle, except on Sundays ; but she got through a great deal of work. On Sundays she put on, with her best gown, an air of calm dignity which made her unhappy until it was off, which it was directly after the evening service. She seemed a very sensible woman, and whatever the merits of the case she sided always with the weakest. The next morning we asked how it was she appeared not to expect us, as I had written and posted the letter myself on the previous Saturday.

"For sure now," she replied, "and the papper scrawl coom'd on Monday; but us bain't girt scholards, and Varmer said most like 'twas the Queen's taxes, for there was her head upon it; so us put un in the big mortar till Beany Dawe should come over, or us should go to church next Zunday, and passon would discoorse it for us. But "—and off she ran—" But her belongs to you now, Miss Clerer, seeing as how you've coom after un."

So they had only a general idea that we were coming, and knew not when it would be. The following day, Thomas Henwood arrived, bringing our boxes in a vehicle called a "butt," which is a short and rudely made cart, used chiefly for carrying lime.

After unpacking our few embellishments, we set up a clumsy but comfortable sofa for my mother, and tried to divert her sadness a little by many a shift and device to garnish our narrow realm. We removed the horrible print of "Death and the Lady," which was hung above the chimneypiece, and sundry daubs of our Lord and the Apostles, and a woman of Samaria with a French parasol, and Eli falling from a turnpike gate over the Great Western steamer. But these alterations were not made without some wistful glances from poor Mrs. Huxtable. At last, when I began to nail up a simple sketch of the church at Vaughan St. Mary instead of a noble representation of the Prodigal Son, wearing a white hat with a pipe stuck under the riband, and weeping into a handkerchief with some horse upon it, the good dame could no longer repress her feelings.

"Whai, Miss Clerer, Miss, dear art alaive, cheel, what be 'bout? Them's the smartest picters anywhere this saide of Coom. Varmer gied a pan of hogs' puddens for they, and a Chainey taypot and a Zunday pair of corderahoys. Why them'll shaine with the zun on 'um, laike a vield of poppies and charlock. But thic smarl pokey papper of yourn ha'ant no more colour nor the track of a marly scrarly. A massy on us if I couldn't walk a better picter than thic, with my pattens on in the zider squash."

To argue with such a connoisseur would have been worse than useless; so I pacified her by hanging the rejected gems in her own little summer room by the dairy. Our parlour began before long to look neat and even comfortable. Of course the furniture was rough, but I care not much for upholstery, and am quite rude of French polish. My only fear was lest the damp from the lime-ash floor should strike to my dear mother's feet, through the scanty drugget which covered it. The fire-place was bright and quaint, lined with old Dutch tiles, and the grey-washed walls were less offensive to

the eye than would have been a paper chosen by good
Mrs. Huxtable. The pretty lattice window, budding
even now with woodbine, and impudent to the winds
with myrtle, would have made amends for the meanest
room in England. Before it lay a simple garden with
sparry walks and bright-thatched hives, and down a
dingle rich with trees and a crystal stream, it caught a
glimpse of the Bristol Channel.

CHAPTER XIV.

WHEN our things were nearly settled, and I was sitting by myself, with dirty hands and covered with dust, there came a little timid tap at the door, followed by a shuffling outside, as if some one contemplated flight, yet feared to fly. Opening the door, I was surprised to find the child whom I expected a massive figure, some six feet and a quarter high, and I know not how many feet in width, but wide enough to fill the entire passage. He made a doubtful step in advance, till his great open-hearted face hung sheepishly above my head.

"Have I the pleasure of seeing Mr. Huxtable?" I asked.

"Ees 'um," he stammered, blushing like a beet-root, "leastways Miss, I ort to zay, no plasure 'um to the laikes of thee, but a honour to ai. Varmer Uxtable they karls me round about these 'ere parts, and some on 'em

Varmer Jan, and Beany Dawe, he karl me 'Varmer Brak-plew-harnish, as tosses arl they Carnish,' and a dale he think of his potry as it please God to give 'un : but Maister, may be, is the riglar thing, leastways you knows best, Miss." "Danged if I can coom to discourse with girt folks nohow, no more nor a sto-un." This was an "aside," but audible a long way off, as they always are on the stage.

"But I am a very small folk, Mr. Huxtable, compared at least with you."

"I humbly ax your parding, Miss, but ai didn't goo for to be zuch a beg, nockety, sprarling zort of a chap. I didn't goo for to do it nohow. Reckon 'twar my moother's valt, her were always draming of hayricks." This also was an "aside."

"Come in," I said, "I am very glad to see you, and so will my mother be."

"Noo! Be e now? Be e though undade, my dear?" he asked with the truest and finest smile I ever saw; and I felt ashamed in front of the strong simplicity which took my conventional words for heart's truth.

"Them's the best words," he continued "as ai 've

'cered this many a dai; for ai'll be danged if ever a loi could coom from unner such eyes as yourn."

And thereupon he took my puny weak hand in his rough iron palm, like an almond in the nut-crackers, and examined it with pitying wonder.

" Wull, wull ! some hands be made for mulking coos, and some be made of the crame itself. Now there couldn't be such a purty thing as this ere, unless it wor to snow war'rm.   But her bain't no kaind of gude for rarstling ? and ai be aveared thee'll have to rarstle a rare bout wi the world, my dearie : one down, tother coom on, that be the wai of 'un."

" Oh, I am not afraid, Mr. Huxtable."

He took some time to meditate upon this, and shook his head when he had finished.

" Noo, thee bain't aveard yet I'll warr'ne.   Gude art alaive, if e bain't a spurrity maid. But if ere a chap zays the black word on e—and thiccy's the taime when a maid can't help herzell, then ony you karl Jan Uxtable that's arl my dear, and if so be it's in the dead hoor of the naight, and thee beest to tother zaide of Hexymoor, ai'll be by the zaide of thee zooner nor ai could thraw a vorchip."

Before I could thank him for his honest championship my mother entered the room, and all his bashfulness (lost for the moment in the pride of strength) came over him again like an extinguisher. Although he did not tremble—his nerves were too firm for that—he stood fumbling with his hat, and reddening, and looking vaguely about, at a loss where to put his eyes or anything else.

My mother, quite worn out with her morning's walk, surprised at her uncouth visitor, and frightened perhaps at his bulk, sank on our new-fangled sofa, in a stupor of weakness. Then it was strange and fine to see the strong man's sense of her feeble state. All his embarrassment vanished at once; he saw there was something to do; and a look of deep interest quickened his great blue eyes. Poising his heavy frame with the lightness of a bird, he stepped to her side as if the floor had been holy, and, scarcely touching her, contrived to arrange the rude cushions, and to lay her delicate head in an easy position, as a nurse composes a child. All the while, his looks and manner expressed so much feeling and gentleness, that he must have known what it was to lose a daughter or mother.

"Poor dear leddy," he whispered to me, "her be used to zummut more plum nor thiccy, I reckon. Her zimth crule weist and low laike. Hath her been long in that there wai?"

"Yes, she has long been weak and poorly; but I fear that her health has been growing worse for the last few months." I couldn't help crying a little; and I couldn't help his seeing it.

"Dang thee, Jan Uxtable, for a doilish girt zinny. Now doon e tak on so, Miss; doon e, that's a dear. Avore her's been here a wake, her'll be as peart as a gladdy. There bain't in arl they furren parts no place the laike of this ere to make a body ston up-raight. The braze cooms off o Hexymoor as frash as a young coolt, and up from the zay as swate as the breath of a coo on the clover, and he'll zit on your chake the zame as a dove on her nestie; and ye'll be so hearty the both on ye, that ye'll karl for taties and heggs and crame and inyons avore e be hout of bed. Ee's fai ye wull." With this homely comfort he departed, after a cheering glance at my mother.

Before I proceed, the Homeric epithet "Break-plough-harness," applied by the poet to Mr. Huxtable, needs some explanation. It appears that the farmer, in some convivial hour (for at other times he detested vaunting), had laid a wager that he and Timothy Badcock, his farm-labourer, would plough half an acre of land, "wiout no beastessy in the falde." Now, it happened that the Parracombe blacksmith had lately been at Barnstaple, and there had seen a man who had heard of ploughing by steam. So when the farmer's undertaking got noised abroad and magnified, all Exmoor assembled to witness the exploit, wondering, trembling, and wrathful. Benches and tables were set in the "higher Barton," a nice piece of mealy land, just at the back of the house, while Suke and Mrs. Huxtable plied the cider-barrel for the yeomen of the neighbourhood. The farmer himself was not visible—no plough or ploughing tackle of any description appeared, and a rumour began to spread that the whole affair was a hoax, and the contriver afraid to show himself. But as people began to talk of "sending for the constable" (who, of course was there all the time), and as cart-whips and knobsticks began to vibrate ominously, Mrs. Huxtable made a signal to Mr. Dawe, who led off the grumbling throng to the further end of the field, where an old rick-cloth lay along against the hedge. While the tilting was moved aside, the bold sons of Exmoor shrunk back, expecting some horrible monster, whose smoke was already puffing. All they saw was a one-horse plough with the farmer, in full harness, sitting upon it and smoking his pipe, and Timothy Badcock patiently standing at the plough-tail. Amid a loud hurrah from his friends, Mr. Huxtable leaped to the fore, and cast his pipe over the hedge; then settled the breast-band across the wrestling-pads on his chest, and drew tight both the chain-traces. "Gee wugg now, if e wull," cried stout Tim Badcock cheerily, and off sailed the good ship of husbandry, cleaving a deep bright furrow. But when they reached the corner, the farmer turned too sharply, and snapped the off-side trace. That accident impressed the multitude with a deeper sense of his prowess than even the striking success which attended his primitive method of speeding the plough.

To return to my mother. As spring came on, and the beautiful country around us freshened and took green life from the balmy air, I even ventured to hope that the good yeoman's words would be true. He had become, by this time, a great friend of ours, doing his utmost that we might not feel the loss of our faithful Thomas Henwood.

Poor Thomas had been very loth to depart; but I found, as we got settled, that my mother ceased to want him, and it would have been wrong as well as foolish to keep him any longer. He invested his savings in a public-house at Gloucester, which he called the "Vaughan Arms," and soon afterwards married Jane Hiatt, a daughter of our head game-keeper; or I ought to say, Mr. Vaughan's.

Ann Maples remained with us still. We lived, as may be supposed, in the most retired manner. My time was chiefly occupied in attendance upon dear mother, and in attempts to create for her some of those countless comforts, whose value we know not until they are lost. After breakfast, my mother would read for an hour her favourite parts of Scripture, and vainly endeavour to lead me into the paths of peace. Her soul discarded more and more the travel garb and wayfaring troubles of this lower existence, as, day by day, it won a nearer view of the golden gate, and the glories beyond; with which I have seen her eyes suffused, like the lucid heaven with sunrise. It has been said, and I believe, that there is nothing, in all our material world, so lovely as a fair woman looking on high for the angels she knows to be waiting for her.

Even I, though looking in an opposite direction, and for an opposite being, could not but admire that gentle meekness, whose absence formed the main fault of my character. Not that I was hard-hearted, or cross, (unless self-love deceives me), but restless yearning and hatred were ever at work within me ; and these repel things of a milder nature, as a bullet cries tush to the zephyr.

CHAPTER XV.

ONE cold day in March, when winter had come to say "good-bye" with a roar, after wheeling the sofa with my mother upon it towards the parlour fire, I went out to refresh my spirit in the kitchen with Mrs. Huxtable, and to "yat myself" (for the sofa took all the parlour fire) by the fragrant hearth of wood and furze. The farmer's wife was "larning" me some strange words of her native dialect, which I was now desirous to "discoorse," and which she declared to be "the only vitty talk. Arl the lave of thiccy stoof, zame as the Carnishers and the Zummersets and the Lunnoners tulls up, arl thiccy's no more nor a passel of gibbersh, Miss Clerer, and not vitty atarl; noo, nor English nother. Instead of zaying 'ai' laike a Kirsten, zome on em zays 'oi,' and zome on em 'I.'" In the middle of her lecture, and just as I had learned that to "quilty" is the proper English for to "swallow," and that the passage down which we quilty is, correctly speaking, not the throat, but the "czelpipe," a strange-looking individual darkened the "draxtool" (corruptly called the threshold) and crossed the "planch," or floor, to the fireplace where we sat.

Turning round, I beheld a man about fifty years old, of moderate stature, gauntly bodied, and loosely built, and utterly reckless of his attire. His face was long and thin, the profile keenly aquiline; and the angles made yet sharper, by a continual twitching and tension of the muscles. The skin of his cheeks was drawn, from his solemn brows to his lipless and down-curved mouth, tight and hollow, like the bladder on a jam-pot. His eyes, of a very pale blue, seemed always to stand on tip-toe, and never to know what he was going to say. A long, straight, melancholy chin, grisly with patches of hair, was meant by nature to keep his mouth shut, and came back sullenly when it failed. Over his shoulders was flung a patched potato-sack, fastened in front with a wooden skewer, and his nether clothes were as ragged as poetry. In his air and manner, self-satisfaction strove hard with solemn reserve. Upon the whole he reminded me of an owl who has lost his heart to a bantam hen. I cannot express him justly; but those who have seen may recognise Beany Dawe, the sawyer, acknowledged the bard of the north of Devon.

Mr. Ebenezer Dawe, without any hesitation or salute, took a three-legged stool, and set it between our chairs, then looked from Mrs. Huxtable to me, and introduced himself.

> "Wull, here be us three,
> And I hopps us shall agree."

"Agray indeed," cried Mrs. Huxtable, "doon 'e zee the quarlity be here, ye aul vule?" Then turning to me. "Doon'e be skeared, Miss Clerer, it be oney that there aul mazed ramscallion, Beany Dawe. Her makth what girt scholards, laike you, karls potry, or zum such stoof. Her casn' oppen the drort of him nohow, but what her must spake potry. Pote* indeed! No tino, I'd pote un out of ouze if I was the waife of un. 'Zee zaw, Beany Dawe!' that be arl the name he hath airned vor his rhaiming and rubbish, and too good for 'un too! Rhaime, rhaime, drash, drash, like two girt gawks in a barn! Oh fai, oh fai; and a maight have airned two zhillings a dai and his zider!"

The subject of these elegant strictures regarded her

* "Pote." Damnonic for to "kick."

all the time, with that pleased pity which none but a
great Poet so placed can feel. Then swinging slowly
on his tripod, and addressing the back of the chimney,
he responded :

> "Poor vule ! Her dunno what a saight 'tis haigher
>   To be a Pöut, nor a hunderzawyer ! "

Perhaps his lofty couplet charmed her savage ear ; at
any rate she made a peaceful overture.

"Coom now, Mr. Dawe, wull e have a few broth ?"

He assented with an alacrity much below his dignity ;

> "Taties, and zider, maat, and broth a few,
>   Wull, zin you ax ai, ai'll not answer noo."

"E shan't have no cider," replied his hostess, " without
e'll spake, for wance, laike a Kirsten, maind that, without no moor of thiccy jingle jangle, the very zame for
arl the world as e be used to droon in the zawpit.
' Zee, zaw, Margery Daw,' with the arms of e a gwayn
up and doon, up and doon, and your oyes and maouth
most chokked with pilm * and the vace of e a hurning
laike a taypot, and never a drop of out to aise the
crickles of your barck. That's the stect you potes be
in, and zawyers."

As she delivered this comment, she swung to and

* Pilm, Londinicè, "dust."

fro on her chair, in weak imitation of the impressive
roll, with which he enforced his rhyme. This plagiarism
annoyed him much more than her words: but he vin-
dicated his cause, like a true son of song.

> " And if zo hap, I be a pöut grand,
>   Thee needn't jah, 'cos thee doon't understand.
>   A pöut, laike a 'ooman, or a bell,
>   Must have his clack out, and can't help hiszell."

A mighty " ha ha " from the door, like a jocund
earthquake, proved that this last hit had found an echo
in some ample bosom.

" Thee shall have as much vittels as ever thee can
let down," said the farmer, as he entered, " danged
if thee bain't a wunnerful foine chap, zure enough.
Ai'd as lieve a'most to be a pote, plase God, as I wud
to be a ooman: zimth to ai, there bain't much differ
atwixt 'em. But they vainds out a saight of things
us taks no heed on. I reckon now, Beany, thee cas'n
drink beer ? "

This was a home thrust, for Mr. Dawe was a notorious drinker. He replied with a heavy sigh and
profoundly solemn look :

> " Ah noo ! a noo ! Unless when I be vorced,
>   By rason, Dactor zaith, my stommick ba'in exhaust."

"And what was it the doctor said to you, Mr. Dawe?"
I asked, perceiving that he courted inquiry. He fixed
his eyes upon me, with a searching look; eager, as it
seemed, yet fearing to believe that he had found at
last a generous sympathy.

> " ' Twas more nor dree months zince ai titched a drap,
> When ai was compelled to consult the Dactor chap ;
> He zaith, zaith he, ' 'tain't no good now this here,
> Oh, Ebenezer Dawe, you *must* tak beer.' "

These words he repeated with impressive earnestness,
shaking his head and sighing, as if in deprecation of
so sad a remedy. Yet the subject possessed perhaps
a melancholy charm, and his voice relented to a pensive
unctuousness, as he concluded.

> " ' Tak beer !' I zays, ' Lor, I dunnow the way !'
> ' Then you must larn,' zays he, ' this blessed day :
> You'm got,' he zays, ' a daungerous zinking here,
> Your constitooshun do requaire beer.' "

"Thee wasn' long avore thee tried it, I'll warr'n,"
said the farmer, "tache the calf the wai to the coo !"

Scorning this vile insinuation, Mr. Dawe continued
thus :

> " Wull, after that, mayhap a month or zo,
> I was gooin home, the zame as maight be noo :

> I had zawed a hellum up for Varmer Yeo,
> And a velt my stommick gooin turble low,
> Her cried and skooned, like a chield left in the dark,
> And a maze laike in my head, and a maundering in my barck.
> Zo whun ai coom to the voot of Breakneck hill,
> I zeed the public kept by Pewter Will:
> The virelight showed the glasses in the bar,
> And 'um danced and twinkled like the avening star."

Here he paused, overcome by his own description.

"Wull," said the farmer, brightening with fellow-feeling, for he liked his glass, "Wull, thee toorned in and had a drap, laike a man, and not be shamed of it nother. And how did her tast? A must have been nation good, after so long a drouth!"

> "Coom'd down my drort, like the Quane and Princess Royal,
> The very sa-am as a drap of oi-al!"

"The very sa-am, the very sa-am," he repeated with an extrametrical smack of his lips, which he wiped with the back of his hand, and cast a meaning glance towards the cellar. The farmer rose, and took from the dresser a heavy quart cup made of pewter. With this he went to the cellar, whence issued presently a trickling and frothing sound, which thrilled to the sensitive heart of Mr. Dawe. The tankard of ale, with a crown of white foam, was presented to the thirsty bard by his host, who did not, however, relinquish his grasp upon the vessel; but imposed (like Pluto to Orpheus) a stern condition. "Now, Beany Dawe, thee shan't have none, unless thee can zay zummut without no poetry in it."

At this barbarous restriction, poor Ebenezer rolled his eyes in a most tragic manner; he thrust his tongue into his cheek, and swung himself, not to and fro as usual, but sideways, and clutched one hand on the tatters of his sack, while he clung with the other to the handle of the cup. Then with a great effort, and very slowly, he spoke—

> "If my poor vasses only maks you frown,
> I'll try, ees fai I wull, to keep 'em—"

A rhyme came over him, the twitching of his face showed the violence of the struggle; he attempted to say "in," but nature triumphed, and he uttered the fatal "down." In a moment the farmer compressed his mighty fingers, and crushed the thick metal like silver paper. The forfeit liquor flew over the poet's knees, and hissed at his feet in the ashes. Foreseeing a storm of verse from him, and of prose from Mrs.

Huxtable at the fate of the pride of her dresser, I made a hasty retreat.

Thenceforth I took a kind interest in our conceited but harmless bard. His neighbours seemed not to know, how long it was since he had first yielded to his unfortunate ailment; which probably owed its birth to the sound of the saw. During our first interview, his rhythm and rhyme had been unusually fluent and finished, from pride perhaps at having found a new audience, or from some casual inspiration. Candour compels me to admit that his subsequent works were little, if at all, better than those of his more famous contemporaries; and I am not so proud, as he expects me to be, of his connexion with my sad history.

CHAPTER XVI.

ABOUT half a mile from Tossil's Barton (the farm-house where we lived) there is a valley, or rather a vast ravine, of a very uncommon formation. A narrow winding rocky combe, where slabs, and tors, and boulder stones, seem pasturing on the velvet grass, or looking into the bright trout-stream, which leaps down a flight of steps without a tree to shade its flash and foam ; this narrow, but glad dingle, as it nears the sea, bursts suddenly back into a desert gorge, cleaving the heights that front the Bristol Channel. The mountain sides from right and left, straight as if struck by rule, steeply converge, like a high-pitched roof turned upside down; so steep indeed that none can climb them. Along the deep bottom gleams a silver chord, where the cramped stream chafes its way, bedded and banked in stone, without a blade of green.

From top to bottom of this huge ravine there is no growth, no rocks, no cliffs, no place to stay the foot, but all a barren, hard, grey stretch of shingle, slates, and gliddery stones: as if the ballast of ten million fleets had been shot in two enormous piles, and were always on the slip. Looking at it we forget that there is such a thing as life: the desolation is not painful, because it is so grand. The brief noon glare of the sun on these Titanic dry walls, where even a lichen dies; the gaunt desert shade stealing back to its lair in the early afternoon; the solemn step of evening stooping to her cloak below—I know not which of these is the most impressive and mournful. No stir of any sort, no voice of man or beast, no flow of tide, ever comes to visit here; the little river, after a course of battles, wins no peaceful union with the sea, but ponds against a shingle bar, and gurgles away in slow whirl-pools. Only a fitful moaning wind draws up and down the melancholy chasm. The famous "Valley of Rocks," some four miles to the east, seems to me common-place and tame compared to this grand defile. Yet how many men I know who would smoke their pipes throughout it!

K 2

Thinking so much of this place, I long wished my mother to see it; and finding her rather stronger one lovely April morning, I persuaded her forth, embarked on Mrs. Huxtable's donkey. We went, down a small tributary glen, towards the head of the great defile. The little glen was bright, and green, and laughing into bud, and bantering a swift brook, which could hardly stop to answer, but left the ousels as it passed to talk at leisure about their nests, and the trout to make those musical leaps that sound so crisp through the alders. Another stream meets it among the bushes below, and now they are entitled to the dignity of a bridge whereon grows the maidenhair fern, and which, with its rude and pointed arch, looks like an old pack-saddle upon the stream.

From this point we followed a lane, leading obliquely up the ascent, before the impassable steep begins. Having tethered our quiet donkey to a broken gate, I took my mother along a narrow path through the thicket to the view of the great ravine. Standing at the end of this path, she was astonished at the scene before her. We had gained a height of about two hundred feet, the hill-top stretched a thousand feet above us. We stood on the very limit of vegetation, a straight line passing down the hill where the quarry-like steep begins.

My dear mother was tired, and I had called her to come home, lest the view should make her giddy ; when suddenly she stepped forward to gather a harebell straggling among the stones. The shingle beneath her foot gave way, then below her, and around, and above her head, began in a great mass to glide. Buried to the knees and falling sideways, she was sinking slowly at first, then quickly and quicker yet, with a hoarse roar of moving tons of stone, gathering and whelming upon her, down the rugged abyss. Screaming, I leaped into the avalanche after her, never thinking that I could only do harm. Stronger, and swifter, and louder, and surging, and berged with shouldering stone the solid cascade rushed on. I saw dearest mother below me trying to clasp her hands in prayer, and to give me her last word. With a desperate effort dragging my shawl from the gulfing crash, I threw it towards her, but she did not try to grasp it. A heavy stone leaped over me, and struck her on the head ; her head dropped back, she lay senseless, and nearly buried. We were dashing more headlong and headlong, in the rush of the mountain side, to the precipice over the river, and my senses had all but failed, and revenge was prone before judgment, when I heard through the din a shout. On the brink of firm ground stood a man, and signed me to throw my shawl. With all my remaining strength I did so, but not as he meant, for I cast it entirely to him, and pointed to my mother below. One instant the avalanche paused, he leaped about twenty feet down, through the heather and gorse, and stayed his descent by clutching a stout ash sapling. To this in a moment he fastened my shawl, (a long and strong plaid), and just as my mother was being swept by, he plunged with the other end into the shingle tide. I saw him leap and struggle towards her, and lift her out of the gliding tomb, gliding himself the while, and sway himself and his burden, by means of the shawl, not back (for that was impossible), but obliquely downwards; I saw the strong sapling bow to the strain like a fishing-rod, while hope and terror fought hard within me; I saw him, by a desperate effort, which bent the ash-tree to the ground, leap from the whirling havoc, and lay my mother on the dead fern and heath. Of the rest, I know nothing, having become quite unconscious, before he saved me, in the same manner.

We must have been taken home in Farmer Huxtable's butt, for I remember well that, amidst the stir and fright of our return, and while my mother was still insensible, Mrs. Huxtable fell savagely upon poor Suke, for having despatched that elegant vehicle without cleaning it from the lime dust; whereby, as she declared, our dresses (so rent and tattered by the jagged stones) were " muxed up to shords." Poor Suke would have been likely to fare much worse, if, at such a time, she had stopped to dust the cart.

When the farmer came home, his countenance, rich in capacity for expressing astonishment, far outdid his words. " Wull, wull, for sure! wuther ye did or no?" was all the vent he could find for his ideas during the rest of the day; though it was plain to all who knew him that he was thinking profoundly upon the subject, and wholly occupied with it. In the course of the following week he advised me very impressively never to do it again ; and nothing could ever persuade him but that I jumped in, and my mother came to rescue me.

But his wife very soon had all her wits about her. She sent to " Coom " for the doctor (I begged that it might not be Mr. Dawe's physician), she put dear mother to bed, and dressed her wounds with simples worth ten druggists' shops, and bathed her temples with rosemary, and ran down the glen for "fathery ham " (Valerian), which she declared " would kill nine sorts of infermation ; " then she hushed the entire household, permitting no tongue to move except her own, and beat her eldest boy (a fine young Huxtable) for crying, whereupon he roared ; she even conquered her strong desire to know much more than all could tell ; and showed my mother such true kindness and pity that I loved her for it at once, and ever since.

Breathing slowly and heavily, my poor mother lay in the bed which had long been the pride of Tossil's Barton. The bedstead was made of carved oak, as many of them are in North Devon, and would have been handsome and striking, if some ancestral Huxtable had not adorned it with whitewash. But the quilt was what they were proud of. It was formed of patches of diamond shape and most incongruous colours, with a death's head in the centre and cross-bones underneath.

When first I beheld it, I tossed it down the stairs, but my mother would have it brought back and used, because she knew how the family gloried in it, and she could not bear to hurt their feelings.

One taper white hand lay on it now, with the tender skin bruised and discoloured by blows. She had closed the finger which bore her wedding ring, and it still remained curved and rigid. In an agony of tears, I knelt by the side of the bed, watching her placid and deathlike face. Till then I had never known how strongly and deeply I loved her.

I firmly believe that she was revived in some degree by the glare of the patched quilt upon her eyes. The antagonism of nature was roused, and brought home her wandering powers. Feebly glancing away, she came suddenly to herself, and exclaimed:

"Is she safe? is she safe?"

"Yes, mother; here I am, with my own dear mother."

She opened her arms, and held me in a nervous cold embrace, and thanked God, and wept.

CHAPTER XVII.

WHEN the surgeon came, he pronounced that none of her limbs were broken, but that the shock to the brain, and the whole system, had been so severe, that the only chance of recovery consisted in perfect quiet. She herself said that the question was, whether Providence wanted her still to watch over her child.

After some days she came down stairs, not without my support, and was propped once more upon her poor sofa.   Calm she appeared, and contented, and happy in such sort as of old; but whenever she turned her glance from me, she observed with starting eyes every little thing that moved. Especially she would lie and gaze through the open window, at a certain large spider, who worked very hard among the woodbine blossoms. One day, in making too bold a cast, he fell; some chord of remembrance was touched, and she swooned away on the couch.

In spite of these symptoms I fondly hoped that she was recovering strength. She even walked out with me twice, in the sunny afternoon. But this only lasted a very short time; it soon became manifest, even to me, that ere long she would be with my father.

Unable to fight any more with this dark perception, I embraced it with a sort of savage despair, an utter sinking of the heart, which defied God as it sank. This she soon discovered, and I fear that it saddened her end.

She was much disappointed, too, that we could not find or thank him who had perilled his life for us. None could tell who he was, or what had become of him; though the farmer, at our entreaty, searched all the villages round. We were told, indeed, by the landlady of the "Red-deer Inn" (a lonely public-house near the scene of the accident) that a stranger had come to her in very great haste, and, having learned who we were, for she had seen us pass half an hour before, had sent her boy to the farm for some kind of conveyance, while he returned at full speed to attend those whom he had rescued. It further appeared that this stranger had helped to place us in the cart, and showed the kindest anxiety to lessen the roughness of its motion, himself even leading old "Smiler," to thwart his propensity to the deepest and hardest ruts. By the time our slow vehicle reached the farm, Mrs. Huxtable was returned from the Lower Cleve orchard, where she had been smoking the fernwebs, in ignorance of our mishap; and our conductor, seeing us safe in her hands, departed without a word, while she was too flurried and frightened to take much notice of him.

Neither could the woman of the inn describe him; she was so "mazed," when she heard of the "vall arl down the girt goyal," as she called our slide of about fifty feet; and for this she quoted the stranger as her authority, "them's the very words as he used;" though, just before this, she had stated that he was a foreigner and could not speak English. Knowing that in Devonshire any stranger is called a foreigner, and English means the brogue of the countryside, I did not attach much weight to this declaration. The only remaining witness, the lad who had come with the butt, was too stupid to describe anything, except three round O's, with his mouth and eyes.

But it mattered little about description; I had seen

that stranger under such circumstances, that I could not fail to know him again.

On the morrow, and once in the following week, some kind inquiries were made as to our condition, by means of slips of paper conveyed by country lads. No name was attached to these, and no information given about the inquirer. The bearer of the first missive came from Lynmouth, and of the second from Ilfracombe. Neither lad knew anything (though submitted by Mrs. Huxtable to keen cross-examination), except that he was paid for his errand, but would like some cider, and that the answer was to be written upon the paper he brought.

Whether any motive for concealment existed, beside an excess of delicacy, or whether there even was any intentional secresy, or merely indifference to our gratitude, was more than we could pretend to say. I am not at all inquisitive—not more so, I mean, than other women—but I need not confess that my curiosity (to say nothing of better feelings) was piqued a little by this uncommon reserve.

So now, beside the engrossing search for my deadly enemy, I had to seek out another, my brave and noble friend.

CHAPTER XVIII.

But for the present, curiosity, gratitude, hate, all
feelings indeed and passions, except from the bled vein
of love, and the heart-rooted fibres of sorrow, were to
be crushed within me. Evening after evening, my dear
mother's presence seemed more and more dreamy and
shadowy; and night after night she went feebler and
feebler to bed. In the morning indeed she had gathered
some fragile strength, such strength as so wasted a form
could exert, and the breeze and the fresh May sun made
believe of health on her cheeks. But no more was I
tempted to lay my arm round her waist, and rally her on
its delicate girlish span, nor could I now look gaily into
her eyes, and tell her how much she excelled her child.
Those little liberties, which with less than a matron's
dignity, and more than a mother's fondness she had so
long allowed me, became as she still expected, and I
could not bear to take them, so many great distresses.

Even at night, when I twined in its simple mode her soft brown hair, as I thought how few the times my old task would be needed again, it cost me many a shift to prevent her descrying my tears in the glass, or suspecting them in my voice. For herself, she knew well what was coming; she had learned how soon she must be my sweet angel instead of my mother, and her last trouble was that she could not bring me to think the difference small. So calmly she spoke of her end, not looking at me the while for fear we both should weep, so gently and sweetly she talked of the time when I should hearken no more, as if she were going to visit a garden and hand me the flowers outside. Then, if I broke forth in an anguish of sobs, she would beg my forgiveness, as if she could have done wrong, and mourn for my loneliness after her, as though she could help forsaking me.

Looking back, even now, on that time, how I condemn and yet pardon myself, reflecting how little I tried to dissemble my child-like woe.

When all things rejoiced in their young summer strength, and scarcely the breeze turned the leaves for the songs of the birds, and the pure white hawthorn was calm as the death of the good, and the soul of gladness was sad, we talked for the last time together, mother and child, looking forth on the farewell of sunset. The room under the thatch smelled musty in summer, and I had made up a bed on the sofa downstairs. The wasting low fever was past, and the wearisome cough exhausted, and the flush had ebbed from her cheeks (as the world from her heart), and of all human passions, and wishes, and cares, not one left a trace in her bosom, except a mother's love. This and only this retarded her flight to heaven, as the sight of his nest delays the rising of the lark.

"My child," she began, and her voice was low, but very distinct, "my only and darling child, who has minded me so long, and laid her youth, and beauty, and high courageous spirit, at the feet of her weak mother; my child, who fostered in wealth and love, will be to-morrow an orphan, cast upon the wide world"—here she fairly broke down, in spite of religion, and heaven, and turned her head to the pillow, a true daughter and mother of earth. I would fain have given that fortune, whose loss to me she lamented, for leave to cry freely with her, without adding to her distress.

In a minute or two, she was able to proceed; with her thin hand she parted the hair shaken purposely over my eyes.

"I am sure that my pet will listen, with kindness and patience, while I try to say what has lain so long at my heart. You know how painfully I have always been moved by any allusion to the death of your dear father. It has been a weakness no doubt on my part, but one which I vainly strove against; and for which I trust to be pardoned where all is pardon and peace."

Her voice began to tremble, and her eyes became fixed, and I feared a return of the old disorder; but she shook it off, and spoke again distinctly, though with great labour:

"This is a bitter subject, and I never could bring myself to it, till now, when it seems too late. But, my poor love, I am so anxious about it. For the rest—that Providence which has never forsaken us, repine as I would, I can trust that Providence still to protect my darling child. There is one thing, and only one, by promising which you will make my departure quite happy. Then I shall go to rejoin your father, and carry such tidings of you, as will enable us both to wait, in the fulness of time, your coming."

"Oh, that the fulness of time were come!" I cried in my selfish loneliness; "for me it is empty enough."

"My precious, my own darling Clara, you sob so, you make me most wretched."

"Mother, I will not cry any more;" neither did I, while she could see me.

"I need not tell you," she said, "what is that promise which I crave for your own dear sake."

"No, ma'am," I replied, "I know quite well what it is."

I saw that I had grieved her. How could I call her then anything else than "mother"?

"My mother dear, you wish me to promise this—that I will forego my revenge upon him who slew my father."

She bowed her head, with a look I cannot describe. In the harsh way I had put it, it seemed as if she were injuring both my father and me.

"Had you asked me anything else, although it were sin against God and man (if you could ask such a thing)—I would have pledged myself to it, as gladly as I would die—die, at least, if my task were done. But this, this one thing only—to abandon what I live for, what I was born to do, to be a traitor to my own father and you—I implore you, mother, by Him whose glory is on you now, do not ask me this."

Her face in its sadness and purity made me bury my eyes and forget things.

" Then I must die, and leave my only child possessed with a murderer's spirit ! "

The depth of her last agony, and which I believed would cling to her even in heaven, was more than I could bear. I knelt on the floor and put my hand to her side. Her worn out heart was throbbing again, with the pang of her disappointment.

" Mother," I cried, " I will promise you this. When I have discovered, as I must do, that man who has made you a widow and me an orphan, if I find any plea whatever to lessen his crime, or penitence to atone for it, as I hope to see my father and mother in heaven, I will try to spare and forgive him. Can you wish me to rest in ignorance, and forget that deed ? "

" Clara," she answered weakly, and she spoke more slowly and feebly every time, " you have promised me all I can hope for. How you loved your father ! Me too you have loved I cannot say how much. For my sake, you have borne poverty, trouble, and illness, without a complaining word. By day, and by night, through my countless wants, and long fretfulness."

I put my finger upon her pale lips. How could she tell such a story then? Her tears came now and then, and would not be stopped, as she laid her weak hand on my head.

"May the God of the fatherless and the poor, who knows and comforts the widow's grief, the God who is taking me now to His bosom, bless with all blessings of earth and heaven, and restore to me this my child."

A sudden happiness fell upon her, as if she had seen her prayer's acceptance. She let her arms fall round me, and laid my cheek by the side of her bright flowing smile. It was the last conscious stir of the mind; all the rest seemed the flush of the soul. In the window the night-scented heath was blooming; outside it, the jessamine crossed in a milky way of white stars, and the lush honeysuckle had flung down her lap in clusters. The fragrance of flowers lay heavy upon us, and we were sore weary with the burden of sorrow and joy. So tranquil and kind was the face of death, that sleep, his half-brother, still held his hand.

The voice of the thrush, from the corner laurel, broke the holy stillness. Like dreams of home that break our slumbers, his melody was its own excuse. My mother awoke, and said faintly, with no gleam in her eyes :

"Raise me upon the pillow, my love, that I may hear him once more. He sings like one your father and I used to listen to every evening, in the days when we watched your cradle."

I lifted her gently. The voice of nature made way for her passing spirit.

"Now kiss me, my child; once more, my own loved child, my heart is with you for ever. Light of my eyes, you are growing dim."

She clasped her hands in prayer, with one of mine between them. My other was round her neck.

Then she spoke slowly, and with a waning voice; but firmly, as if it had been her marriage-response.

"Thou art my guide, and my staff. I have no fear, neither shadow of trembling. Make no long tarrying, oh my God!"

The bird went home to his nest, and she to that

refuge where all is home. Though the hands that held mine grew cold as ice, and her lips replied to no kiss, and the smile on her face slept off into stillness, and a grey shade crept on her features ;—I could not believe that all this was death.

CLARA VAUGHAN.

BOOK II.

CHAPTER I.

" LONG-SHADOWED death," some poet says. How well
I know and feel it! the gloom before him deepening as
he comes, and the world of darkness stretching many
years behind.

I once dared to believe that no earthly blow could
ever subdue, or even bend my resolute will. I now
found my mistake, and cared not even to think about it.

On the morning after my mother's death I wandered
about, and could not tell where to go. The passionate
clinging which would not allow me, during that blank
and sleepless night, to quit what remained of her presence, and the jealous despair which felt it a wrong that
any one else should approach, had now settled down to
a languid heaviness, and all that I cared for was to be
let alone. All the places where we had been together
I visited now, without knowing why, perhaps it was to
see if she were there. Then vaguely disappointed, I

thought there must be some mistake, and wearily went the dreary round again.

I cannot clearly call to mind, but think it must have been that day, when I was in the corner of the room, looking at the place whence they had taken dear mother. Ann Maples and Mrs. Huxtable came in, followed by the farmer, who had left his shoes at the door. They did not see me, so I suppose it must have been in the evening. They were come to remove the sofa. I have not the heart to follow their brogue.

"Yes to be sure," said Mrs. Huxtable, looking at it with a short sigh. It was odd that it should strike me then, but all she did was short.

"Get it out of her sight, poor dear," said Ann Maples.

"To see her sit and look at it!" exclaimed the farmer's wife.

"With her eyes so dry and stupid like!" returned the other. "Poor child, she must have cried herself out. I have known her sit by the hour, and stare at the bed where her father was killed, but it was a different sort of look to this."

"Ah well, she has lost a good mother," said Dame

Huxtable. "God grant my poor little chicks may never be left like her."

"What's your children to talk of along with Miss Clara?" asked my nurse.

Mrs. Huxtable was about to answer sharply, but checked herself, and only said:

"All children is much of a muchness to their mothers."

"Don't tell me," cried Ann Maples, who had never had any.

The farmer came between them, walking on tip-toe.

"For good, now, don't ye fall out at such a time as this here. What's our affairs to speak of now?"

"What's any folks," asked Mrs. Huxtable, "that has the breath of life?"

"And goes forth in the morning, and is cast into the oven, ma'am," continued her antagonist.

"Ah, bless thee, yes!" the farmer replied, "I'll take my gospel oath of it. It's not much good I am at parsoning, and maybe I likes a drop of drink when the weather is fitty; but that young chestnut filly that's just come home from breaking, I'd sell her to a gipsey, and trust him for the money, if so be 'twould make the

young lady turn her face to the Lord. Can't ye speak
to her now about it, either of you women? Doo'e now,
doo'e."

"How could I possible?" his wife exclaimed; "why,
farmer, you must be mazed. A high young lady like
that, and the tears still hot in her eyes!"

"The very reason, wife, the very time and reason.
But likely Mrs. Maples would be the proper person."

"Thank you, sir," my nurse replied, "Mrs. Maples
knows good manners a little. Thank you, sir; Mrs.
Maples wasn't born in Devonshire."

"I ask your pardon, ma'am," said the farmer, much
abashed, "I humbly ask your pardon; I wasn't taught
no better. I can only go by what I have seen, and
what seems to come inside of me. And I know, in our
way of business, when a calf is weaned from the
mother, the poor beastess hath a call for some one
else to feed it. Maybe it's no harm to let her have the
refusal." Therewith he opened my mother's Bible, and
placed it reverently on the window-seat. "Waife, do'e
mind the time as poor Aunt Betsy died, over there to
Rowley Mires?"

"For sure I do, but what have her got to do with it?

Us mustn't talk of her, I reckon, any more than of the chillers, though us be so unlucky as to be born in Devonshire. Fie, fie, thee ought to know better than to talk of poor Aunt Betsy along of a lady, and before our betters." Here she curtsied to Ann Maples, with a flash of light in her eyes, and rubbing them hard with her apron.

" Well, well," replied the farmer, sadly, "mayhap so I did. And who be I to gainsay? Mayhap so I did;" he dropped his voice, but added, after some reflection, " It be hard to tell the rights of it; but sure her were a woman."

" Who said her were a man, thee zany?" Mrs. Huxtable was disappointed that the case would not be argued. The farmer discreetly changed the subject.

" Now, if it was me," he continued, "I wouldn't think of taking this here settle-bed away from the poor thing."

" Why not, farmer?" asked Mrs. Huxtable, sharply. " Give me a reason for leaving it, and I'll give you ten for taking it."

" I can't give no reasons. But maybe it comforts her a little."

" Comfort indeed ! " said his wife ; " breaks her heart

with crying, more likely. Come, lend a hand, old heavy-strap; what can a great dromedary like thee know about young wenches?"

At any rate he knew more than she did. The moment they touched it I burst forth from my corner, and flung myself upon it, rolling as if I would bury myself in the ecstasy of anguish. What they did I cannot tell; they might say what they liked, I had not cried till then.

The next day I was sitting stupified and heavy, trying once more to meet the necessity of thinking about my mother's funeral; but again and again, the weakness of sorrow fell away from the subject. The people of the house kept from me. Mrs. Huxtable had done her best, but they knew I would rather be alone.

The door was opened quietly, and some one entered in a stealthy manner. Regarding it as an intrusion, I would not look that way.

"Miss Clara dear," began the farmer, standing behind me, and whispering, "I humbly ask your pardon, Miss, for calling you that same. But we have had a wonderful fine season, sure enough."

I made him no answer, being angry at his ill-timed common-place.

"If you please, Miss, such a many lambs was never known afore, and turnips fine last winter, and corn, and hay, and every kind of stock, a fetching of such prices. The farmers about here has made their fortune mainly."

"I am glad to hear that you are so prosperous, Mr. Huxtable," I answered, very coldly.

"Yes fie, good times, Miss, wonderful good times, we don't know what to do with our money a'most."

"Buy education and good taste," I said, "instead of thrusting your happiness upon such as I."

How little I knew him! Shall I ever forgive myself that speech?

"Ah, I wish I could," he answered, sadly, "I wish with all my heart I could. But we must be born to the like of that, I am afeared, Miss Vaughan."

Poor fellow! he knew nothing of irony, as we do, who are born to good taste, otherwise I might have suspected him of it then.

He suddenly wished me "good evening," although it was middle-day, and then he made off for the door, but came back again with a desperate resolve, and spoke, for him, very quickly, looking all the time at his feet.

"There, I can't make head or tail of it, Miss Clara, but wife said I was to do it so. Take the danged money, that's a dear, and for good now don't be offended, for I cas'n help it."

He opened his great hand, which was actually shaking, and hurriedly placed on the sofa a small packet tied in the leaf of a copy book; then suddenly put in mind of something, he made a dive, and snatching it up, flung it upon a Windsor chair. It fell with a chink, the string slipped off, and out rolled at least forty sovereigns and guineas, and a number of crown-pieces.

Peremptorily I called him back, for he was running out of the door.

"Mr. Huxtable, what is the meaning of this?"

"Meaning, Miss! Lord bless you, Miss Clara, there bain't no meaning of it; only it comed into my head last night, as I was laying awake, humbly asking your pardon, Miss, for that same, that if so be you should desire, that the dear good lady herself might like, if I may make so bold, meaning that it isn't fitty like, that she should lay nowhere else, but alongside of her own husband, till death do them part, Mr. Henry Valentine Vaughan, Esquire, Vaughan Park, in the county of Gloucestershire. There I be as bad as Beany Dawe."

He repeated his rhyme, with some relief, hoping to change the subject. I caught him by both hands, and burst into tears.

"Don't ye now," he said, with a thickness in his voice, "don't ye now, my dearie, leastways unless it does you good."

"It does me good, indeed," I sobbed, "to find still in the world so kind a heart as yours."

Though I longed to look him in the face, I knew that I must not do so. Oh why are men so ashamed of manly tears? Perceiving that I could not speak, he began to talk for both of us, making a hundred blundering apologies, trying to hide his knowledge of my poverty, and to prove that he was only paying a debt which extended over many years of tenancy. He was not at all an imaginative man, but delicacy supplied him with invention. So deep a sense pervades all classes in this English country, that want of money is an indictment, which none but the culprit may sign. Poor or rich, I should not be worth despising, if I had shown the paltry pride of declining such a loan.

The tears came anew to my eyes when I found that what had been brought so freely was the savings of years of honest toil, a truth which the owners had tried to conceal by polishing the old coin. But not being skilled, dear souls, in plate-cleaning, they had left some rotten-stone adhering to the George and Dragons.

CHAPTER II.

ALTHOUGH I find a sad pleasure in lingering over these times, with such a history still impending, I cannot afford the indulgence.

Dear mother's simple funeral took me once more to my native place. Even without Mr. Huxtable's generous and noble assistance, I should have laid her to rest by the side of the husband she loved so well. But difficulties, sore to encounter at such a time, would have met me on every side. Moreover the kind act cheered and led me through despondency, like the hand and face of God.

Caring little what people might say or think, I could not stay at a distance. Nature told me that it was my duty to go, and duty or not, I could not stay away.

And now for the last time I look on the face and form of my mother. That which I have played, and talked, and laughed with, though lately not much of laughter, that which has fed and cared for me, till it needed my care in turn; that which I have toddled beside, or proudly run in front of; whose arms have been round me whenever I wept, and whose bosom the haven of childhood's storms; first to greet me with smiles in the morning, and last to bless me with tears at night; ever loving, and never complaining—in one word for a thousand, my mother. So far away now, so hopelessly far away! There it lies indeed, I can touch it, kiss it, and embrace it; but oh how small a part of mother! and even that part is not mine. So holy and calm it lies, such loving kindness still upon its features, so near me, but in mystery so hopelessly far away! I can see it, but it never will know me again; I may die beside it, and it cannot weep. The last last look of all on earth—they must have carried me away.

I remember tottering down the hill, supported by a stalwart arm. The approach to the house prevented— or something. Two children ran before me, stopping now and then to wonder, and straggling to pick hedge-flowers. One of them brought me a bunch, then stared, and was afraid to offer them. "Nancy, I'll be the death of thee," whispered a woman's voice. The little girl shrunk to me for shelter, with timid tears in her great blue eyes. So I took her hand, and led her on, and somehow it did me good.

At intervals, the funeral hymn, which they sing on the road to the grave, fell solemnly on our ears. Some one from time to time gave out the words of a verse and then it was sung to a simple impressive tune. That ancient hymn, which has drowned so many sobs, I did not hear, but felt it.

We arrived at Vaughan St. Mary late in the afternoon of the second day. The whole of the journey was to me a long and tearful dream. Mr. Huxtable came with us. He had never before been further from home than Exeter; and his single visit to that city had formed the landmark of his life. He never tried to comfort me as the others did. The ignorant man knew better.

Alone I sat by my father's grave, with my mother's ready before my feet. They had cast the mould on the other side, so as not to move my father's coverlet. The poor old pensioner had been true to her promise, and man's last garden was blooming like his first flower-bed.

My mind (if any I had) seemed to have undergone some change. Defiance, and pride, and savage delight in misery, were entirely gone; and depression had taken the place of dejection. Death now seemed to me the usual and proper condition of things, and I felt it an impertinence that I should still be alive. So I waited, with heavy composure, till she should be brought, who so often had walked there with me. At length she was coming for good and all, and a space was left for me. But I must not repose there yet; I had still my task before me.

The bell was tolling faster, and the shadows growing longer, and the children who had been playing at hide-and-seek, where soon themselves shall be sought in vain, had flitted away from sight, perhaps scared at my presence, perhaps gone home to tea, to enjoy the funeral afterwards. The evening wind had ceased from troubling the yews, and the short-lived songs of the birds were done. The place was as sad as I could wish. The smell of new earth inspired, as it always does, some unsearchable everlasting sympathy between the material and the creature.

The sun was setting behind me: suddenly a shadow

eclipsed my own upon the red loam across the open grave. Without a start, and dreamily (as I did all things now), I turned to see whence it came. Within a yard of me stood Mr. Edgar Vaughan. In a moment the old feeling was at my heart, and my wits were all awake.

I observed that he was paler than when I had seen him last, and the rigid look was wavering on his face, like steel reflected by water. He lifted his hat to me. I neither rose nor spoke, but turned and watched him.

"Clara," he said in a low, earnest voice, "I see you are still the same. Will no depth of grief, no length of time, no visitation from Him who is over us all, ever bend your adamant and implacable will?"

I heard, with some surprise, his allusion to the Great Being, whom he was not wont to recognise; but I made him no reply.

"Very well," he resumed, with the ancient chill hardening over his features; "so then let it be. I am not come to offer you condolence, which you would despise; nor do I mean to be present when you would account the sight of me an insult. And yet I loved your mother, Clara; I loved her very truly."

This he said with such emotion, that a new thought broke upon me.

Quick as the thought, he asked, "Would you know who killed your father?"

"And my mother, too," I answered, "whose coffin I see coming."

The funeral turned the corner of the lane, and the dust rose from the bearers' feet. He took his hat off, and the perspiration stood upon his forehead. Betwixt suspense and terror, and the wildness of grief, I was obliged to lean on the headstone for support, and a giddiness came over me. When I raised my eyes again, there was no one near me. In vain I wiped them hurriedly and looked again. Mr. Vaughan was gone; but on the grass at my feet lay a folded letter. I seized it quickly, and broke the seal. That moment a white figure appeared between the yew-trees by the porch. It was the aged minister leading my mother the last path of all. The book was in his hand, and his form was tall and stately, and his step so slow, that the white hair fell unruffled, while the grand words on his lips called majesty into his gaze. Thrusting aside the letter, I followed into the Church, and stood behind the old font where I had been baptized ; a dark and gloomy nook, fit for such an entrance. She who had carried me there was carried past it now, and the pall waved in the damp cold air, and all the world seemed stone and mould.

But afterwards, on the fair hill-side, while the faint moon gathered power from the deepening sky, and glancing on that hoary brow sealed the immortal promises and smoothed the edges of the grave, around which bent the uncovered heads of many who had mourned before, and after a few bounds of mirth should bend again in mourning, until in earth's fair turn and turn, others should bend and they lie down—beholding this, and feeling something higher than " dust to dust," I grew content to bide my time with the other children of men, and remembered that no wave can break until it reach the shore.

CHAPTER III.

WHEN a long and heavy sleep (my first sleep since dear mother's death) had brought me down to the dull plain of life, I read for the first time the letter so strangely delivered. Even then it seemed unkind to my mother that I should think about it. Mr. Vaughan had placed it in a new envelope, which he had sealed with his own ring, the original cover (if any there were) having been removed. The few words, of which it consisted, were written in a clear round hand, upon a sheet of thin tough paper, such as we use for foreign postage, and folded in a peculiar manner. There was nothing remarkable in the writing, except this, that the words as well as the letters were joined. It was as follows:

"The one who slain your brother is at 19 Grove Street London. You will come in danger of it why you know."

No date, no signature, no stops, except as shown

above. In short, it was so dark and vague, that I returned to Devonshire, with a resolution to disregard it wholly. When we reached the foot of the hill, at the corner of the narrow lane which leads to Tossil's Barton, and where the white gate stands of which the neighbourhood is so proud, a sudden scream was heard, and a rush made upon us from behind the furze-bush. The farmer received the full brunt of a most vigorous onset, and the number and courage of the enemy making up for their want of size, his strong bastions were almost carried by storm. To the cry of "Daddy! Daddy's come home!" half a dozen urchins and more, without distinction of sex, jumped and tugged and flung and clung around him, with no respect whatever for his Sunday coat, or brass-buttoned gaiters. Taking advantage of his laughing, they pulled his legs this way and that, as if he were skating for the first time, and little Sally (his favourite) swarming up, made a base foot-rope of the great ancestral silver watch-chain whose mysterious awe sometimes sufficed to keep her eyes half open in church. Betwixt delight and shame, the poor father was so dreadfully taken aback, that he could not tell what to do, till fatherly love suggested the only escape. He lifted them one by one to his lips, and after some hearty smacks sent all (except the baby) sliding down his back.

While all this was going forward, the good dame, with a clean apron on, kept herself in the background, curtseying and trying to look sad at me, but too much carried away to succeed. Her plump cheeks left but little room for tears, yet I thought one tried to find a road from either eye. When the burst was nearly done, she felt (like a true woman) for me so lonely in all this love, though I could not help enjoying it; and so she tried to laugh at it.

For a long time after this, the farmer was admired and consulted by all the neighbouring parishes, as a man who had seen the world. His labourers, also, one man and a boy, for a fortnight called him "Sir," a great discomfort to him; more than this, some letters were brought for him to interpret, and Beany Dawe became unduly jealous. But in this, as in most other matters, things came to their level, and when it was slowly discovered that the farmer was just the same, his neighbours showed much disappointment, and even some contempt.

It was not long before the thought of that letter, which had been laid by so scornfully, began to work within me. Again and again, as time wore on, and the deep barb of sorrow darkly rusted away, it came home to me as a sin, that I was neglecting a special guidance. Moreover, my reason for staying in Devonshire was gone, and as my spirit recovered its tone, it could not put up with inaction.

Three months after our return, one breezy afternoon in August, when the heath had long succeeded the gorse and broom upon the cleve, and the children were searching for "wuts" and half-kerneled nuts, I sat on a fallen tree, where a break in the copse made a frame for one of our favourite views. Of late I had been trying to take some sketches in water-colours of what my mother and I had so often admired together, and this had been kept for the last. Wild as the scheme may appear to all who know the world and its high contempt for woman's skill, I had some hope of earning money in London by the pencil, and was doing my utmost to advance in art. Also, I wished to take away with me some memorials of a time comparatively happy.

Little Sally Huxtable, a dear little child, now my chief companion, had strayed into the wood to string more strawberry beads on her spike of grass, for the wood strawberries here last almost to the equinox; and I had just roughed in my outline, and was correcting the bold strokes, by nature's soft gradations; when suddenly through a cobnut bush, and down the steep bank at my side, came, in a sliding canter, a magnificent red deer. He passed so close before me, with antlers, like a varnished crabstick, russet in the sun, that I could have touched his brown flank with my pencil. Being in no hurry or fright whatever, he regarded me from his large deep eyes with a look of courteous interest, a dignified curiosity too well bred for words; and then, as if with an evening of pleasant business before him, trotted away through the podded wild broom on the left.

Before I had time to call him back, which, with a childish impulse, I was about to do, the nutbush where he had entered moved again, and, laughing at his own predicament on the steep descent, a young man leaped and landed in the bramble at my feet. Before me stood the one whom we had so often longed to thank. But at sight of me, his countenance changed entirely. The face, so playful just before, suddenly grew dark and sad, and, with a distant salutation, he was hurrying away, when I sprang forward and caught him by the hand. Every nerve in my body thrilled, as I felt the grasp that had saved my mother and me.

"Excuse me," he said coldly, "I will lose my prey."

But I would not let him go so curtly. What I said I cannot tell, only that it was very foolish, and clumsy, and cold by the side of what I felt. Whom but God and him had I to thank for my mother's peaceful end, and all her treasured words, each worth a dozen lives of mine? He answered not at all, nor looked at me; but listened with a cold constraint, and, as I thought, contemptuous pity, at which my pride began to take alarm.

"Sir," I exclaimed, when still he answered not, "Sir, I will detain you no longer from murdering that poor stag."

He answered very haughtily, "I am not of the Devonshire hunters, who toil to exterminate this noble race."

As he spoke he pointed down the valley, where the

red deer, my late friend, was crossing, for his evening browse, to a gnoll of juicy grass. Then why was he pursuing him, and why did he call him his prey? The latter, probably a pretext to escape me, but the former question I could not answer, and did not choose to ask. He went his way, and I felt discharged of half my obligation.

CHAPTER IV.

THE farmer, his wife, and little Sally were now all I had to love. Poor Ann Maples, though thoroughly honest and faithful, was of a nature so dry and precise that I respected rather than loved her. I am born to love and hate with all my heart and soul, although a certain pride prevents me from exhibiting the better passion, except when strongly moved. That other feeling, sown by Satan, he never allows me to disguise.

To leave the only three I loved was a bitter grief, to tell them of my intention, a sore puzzle. But, after searching long for a good way to manage it, the only way I found was to tell them bluntly, and not to cry if it could be helped. So when Mrs. Huxtable came in full glory to try upon me a pair of stockings of the brightest blue ever seen, which she had long been knitting on the sly, for winter wear, I thanked her warmly, and said:

"Dear me, Mrs. Huxtable, how they will admire these in London."

"In Lonnon, cheel!"—she always called me her child, since I had lost my mother—"they'll never see the likes of they in Lonnon, without they gits one of them there long glaskies, same as preventive chaps has, and then I reckon there'll be Hexymoor between, and Dartmoor too, for out I know, and ever so many church-towers and milestones."

"Oh yes, they will. I shall be there in a week."

"In Lonnon in a wake! Dear heart alaive, cheel, dont'e tell on so!"

She thought my wits were wandering, as she had often fancied of late, and set off for the larder, which was the usual course of her prescriptions. But I stopped her so calmly that she could not doubt my sanity.

"Yes, dear Mrs. Huxtable, I must leave my quiet home, where all of you have been so good and kind to me; and I have already written to take lodgings in London."

"Oh, Miss Clerer, dear, I can't belave it nohow! Come and discoorse with farmer about it. He knows a power more than I do, though I says it as shouldn't. But if so be he hearkens to the like of that, I'll comb him with the toasting iron."

Giving me no time to answer, she led me to the kitchen. The farmer, who had finished his morning's work, was stamping about outside the threshold, wiping his boots most carefully with a pitchfork and a rope of twisted straw. This process, to his great discomfort, Mrs. Huxtable had at length enforced by many scoldings; but now she snatched the pitchfork from him, and sent it flying into the court.

"Wun't thee never larn, thee girt drummedary, not to ston there an hour, mucking arl the place?"

"Wull, wull," said the farmer, looking at the pitchfork first, and then at me, "Reckon the old mare's dead at last."

"Cas'n thee drame of nothing but hosses and asses, thee girt mule? Here's Miss Clerer, as was like a cheel of my own, and now she'm gooin awai, and us'll niver zee her no more."

"What dost thee mane, 'ooman?" asked the farmer, sternly, "hast thee darr'd to goo a jahing of her, zame as thee did Zuke?"

"Oh, no, farmer!" I answered, quickly, "Mrs. Huxtable never gave me an unkind word in her life. But I must leave you all, and go to live in London."

The farmer looked as if he had lost something, and began feeling for it in all his pockets. Then, without a word, he went to the fire, and unhung the crock which was boiling for the family dinner. This done, he raked out the embers on the hearthstone, and sat down heavily on the settle with his back towards us. Presently we heard him say to himself, "If any cheel of mine ates ever a bit of bakkon to-day, I'll bile him in that there pot. And to zee the copy our Sally wrote this very morning!"

"Wonnerful! wonnerful!" cried Mrs. Huxtable, "and now her'll not know a p from a pothook. And little Jack can spell zider, zame as 'em does in Lonnon town!"

"Dang Lonnon town," said the farmer, savagely, "and arl as lives there, lave out the Duke of Wellington. It's where the devil lives, and 'em catches his braath in lanterns. My faather tould me that, and her niver spak a loi. But it bain't for the larning I be vexed to lose my dearie."

That last word he dwelt upon so tenderly and sadly,

that I could stop no longer, but ran up to him bravely with the tears upon my face. As I sat low before him, on little Sally's stool, he laid his great hand on my head, with his face turned toward the settle, and asked if I had any one to see me righted in the world but him.

I told him, " None whatever ; " and the answer seemed at once to please and frighten him.

"Then don't e be a-gooin', my dear heart, don't e think no more of gooin. If it be for the bit and drap thee ates and drinks, doesn't thee know by this time, our own flash and blood bain't no more welcome to it ? And us has a plenty here, and more nor a plenty. And if us hadn't, Jan Huxtable hisself, and Honor Huxtable his waife, wud live on pegmale (better nor they desarves) and gie it arl to thee, and bless thee for ating of it."

"Ay, that us wud, ees fai," answered Mrs. Huxtable, coming forward.

" And if it be for channge, and plaisure, and zeeing of the warld, I've zeen a dale in my time, axing your pardon, Miss, for convarsing so to you. And what hath it been even at Coom market, with the varmers I've a-knowed from little chillers up ? No better nor a harrow dill for a little coolt to zuck. I'd liefer know

thee was a-gooin' to Trentisoe churchyard, where little
Jane and Winny be, than let thee goo to Lonnon town,
zame as this here be. And what wud thy poor moother
zay, if so be her could hear tell of it?"

At this moment, when I could say nothing, being
thoroughly convicted of ingratitude, and ashamed before natures far better than my own, dear little Sally,
who had been rolling on the dairy floor, recovered from
the burst of childish grief enough to ask whether it
had any cause. Up to me she ran, with great pearl
tears on the veining of her cheeks, and peeping through
the lashes of her violet-blue eyes, she gave me one long
reproachful look, as if she began to understand the
world, and to find it disappointment; then she buried
her flaxen head in the homespun apron I had lately
taken to wear, and sobbed as if she had spoiled a
dozen copies. What happened afterwards I cannot tell.
Crying I hate, but there are times when nothing else
is any good. I only know that, as the farmer left the
house to get, as he said, " a little braze," these ominous
words came back from the court:

"'Twud be a bad job for Tom Grundy, if her coom'd
acrass me now."

CHAPTER V.

THAT same evening, as I was sitting in my lonely room, yet not quite alone,—for little Sally, who always did as I bade her, was scratching and blotting her best copy-book, under my auspices,—in burst Mrs. Huxtable, without stopping to knock as usual.

"Oh Miss Clerer, what *have* e been and doed? Varmer's in crule trouble. Us'll arl have to goo to gaol to-morrow, chillers and arl."

She was greatly flurried and out of breath, and yet seemed proud of what she had to tell. She did not require much asking, nor beat about the bush, as many women do ; but told me the story shortly, and then asked me to come and hear all particulars from Tim Badcock the farm-labourer, who had seen the whole.

Tim sat by the kitchen fire with a pint of cider by him on the little round table ; strong evidence that his tidings, after all, were not so very unwelcome.

"Wull, you zee, Miss," said Tim, after getting up, and pulling his rough forelock, "you zee, Miss, the Maister coom out this arternoon, in a weist zort of a wai, as if her hadn't had no dinner." Here he gave a sly look at "the Missus," who had the credit of stopping the supplies, when the farmer had been too much on the cruise.

"What odds to thee, Tim," she replied, "what odds to thee, what thee betters has for dinner?"

"Noo fai," said Tim, "zo long as ai gits maine, and my missus arlways has un raddy. Zo I zed to Bill, zays I, 'Best maind what thee's at boy, there's a starm a coomin, zure as my name's Timothy Badcock.' Howsomever her didn't tak on atarl wi we, but kitched up a shivel, and worked awai without niver a ward. 'Twur the tap of the clave, 'langside of the beg fuzz, where the braidle road coomth along 'twixt that and the double hadge; and us was arl a stubbing up the bushes as plaisant as could be, to plough thiccy plat for clover, coom some rain, plase God."

"Git on, Tim, wull e," cried his impatient mistress, "us knows arl about that. Cas'n thee tull it no quicker?"

"Wull, Miss," continued Tim, in no hurry whatever,

"prasently us zees a girt beg chap on a zort of a brown cob, a coomin in our diraction"—Tim was proud of this word, and afraid that we should fail to appreciate it— "they was a coomin, as you might zay, in our diraction this beg chap, and anither chap 'langside on him. Wull, when 'um coom'd within spaking room of us, beg chap a' horsebarck hollers out, 'Can 'e tell, my men, where Jan Uxtable live?' Avore I had.taime to spake, Maister lifts hissell up, and zaith, 'What doo 'e want to know for, my faine feller?' every bit the zame as ai be a tullin of it to you. 'What's the odds to thee,' zays tother chap, 'thee d'st better kape a zivil tongue in thee head. I be Tom Gundry from Carnwall.' And with that he stood up in his starrups, as beg a feller as iver you zee, Miss. Wull, Maister knowed all about Tom Gundry and what a was a coom for, and zo did I, and the boy, and arl the country round; for Maister have gotten a turble name for rarstling; maybe, Miss, you've a heer'd on him in Lunnon town?"

"I have never been in London, Tim, since I was a child; and I know nothing at all about wrestling."

"Wull, Miss, that be nayther here nor there. But there had been a dale of brag after Maister had thrown

arl they Carnishers to Barnstable vair, last year, about
vetching this here Tom Gundry, who wor the best man
in Carnwall, to throw our Maister.　Howsomever, it be
time for ai to crack on a bit.　'Ah,' zays the man
avoot, who zimth had coom to back un, 'ah, 'twor arl
mighty faine for Uxtable to play skittles with our
zecond rate men.　Chappell or Ellicombe cud have
doed as much as that.　Rackon Jan Uxtable wud vind
a different game with Tom Gundry here.'　'Rackon he
wud,' zaith Gundry, 'a had better jine a burial club, if
her've got ere a waife and vamily."

"Noo.　Did a zay that though?" inquired Mrs. Huxtable, much excited.

" 'Coom now,' my maister zaith, trying to look smarl
behaind the fuzz, 'thee must throw me, my lad, avore
thee can throw Jan Uxtable.　He be a better man
mainly nor ai be this dai.　But ai baint in no oomer
for playin' much jist now, and rackon ai should hoort
any man ai kitched on.'　'Hor that be a good un, Zam,
baint it now?' zaith Gundry to little chap, the very zame
as ai be a tullin it now, 'doth the fule s'pose ai be ratten?
Ai've half a maind to kick un over this hadge; jist
thee hold the nag!'　'Sober now,' zaith varmer, and

ai zeed a was gettin' rad in the chakes, 'God knows ai don't feel no carl to hoort 'e. Ai'll gie thee wan chance more, Tom Gundry, as thee'st a coom arl this wai fram Carnwall. Can 'e trod a path in thiccy country, zame as this here be?' And wi' that, a walked into the beg fuzz, twaice so haigh as this here room, and the stocks begger round nor my body, and harder nor wrought hiern. A jist stratched his two hons, raight and left, and twitched un up, wan by wan, vor ten gude lanyard, as asily as ai wud pull spring inyons. 'Now, wull e let me lone?' zaith he, zo zoon as a coom barck, wi his brath a little quicker by rason of the exarcise, 'wull 'e let me lone?' 'Ee's fai, wull I,' zaith the man avoot. 'Hor,'' zaith Tom Gundry, who had been a* shopping zumwhere, 'thee cans't do a gude dai's work, my man, tak that vor thee's wages.' And wi' that a lets fly at Maister's vace wi' a light hash stick a carr'd, maning to raide off avore Maister cud coom to's brath again. In a crack Jan Uxtable zet both his hons under the stommick of the nag, one avore the starrup and one behaind, zame as I maight to this here little tabble, and haved un, harse and man, clane over hadge into Muster

---

* *i.e.* dealing commercially where the staples are liquid.

Yeo's turmot falde.   Then with wan heft, a kitched up
tother chap, and zent un sprarling after un, zame as if
'twor this here stule after the tabble."

I thought poor Tim, in the excitement of his story,
would have thrown table and stool over the settle to
illustrate it ; and if he had, Mrs. Huxtable would have
forgiven him.

" ' Thar,' zaith our Maister, as plaisant as cud be, and
ai thought us shud have died of laffing, ' thar now, if zo
be the owner of thiccy falde zummons e for traspash,
you zay Jan Uxtable zent e on a little arrand, to vaind
a Carnisher as can do the laike to he.'   And wi' that, a
waiped his hons with a slip of vern, and tuk a little
drap of zider, and full to's wark again."

" Wull, but Tim," asked the farmer's wife, to lose no
part of the effect, " what zort of a hadge wor it now ?
Twor a little hadge maybe, no haigher nor the zettle
barck."

" Wor it though ?" said Tim, " thee knows better nor
that, Missus.   It be the beggest hadge on arl the varm,
wi' a double row of saplin hash atap.   Her maks the
boundary betwixt the two parishes, and ain't been
trimmed these vaive year, ai can swear."

"And how be the both on 'em now, Tim? A must have gone haigh enough to channge the mune.

"Wull, Miss," said Tim, addressing me, for he had told his Mistress all the story twice, "Tom Gundry brak his collar boun, and zarve 'un raight, for a brak Phil Dascombe's a puppose whun a got 'un in a trap, that taime down to Bodmin thar; and harse gat a rick of his taial; but the little chap, be vell upon his hat, and that zaved him kindly. But I heer'd down to Pewter Will's, whur I gooed for a drap of zumthin for my waife's stommick, ai heer'd zay there, as how Constable was a coomin to Maister this very naight, if Carnishers cud have perswadded un. But Constable zaith, zaith he, 'Twor all along o you Carnish chaps, fust battery was mad, and fust blow gien, and wi'out you can zhow me Squaire Drake's warrant, I wunt have nout to do wi' it, not ai; and that be law and gospel in Davonsheer and in Carnwall.'"

"Tim," said Mrs. Huxtable, "I'se warrant thee's niver tould so long a spin up in thee's laife avore. And thee's tould it wonnerful well too; hathn't un, Miss Clerer? Zuke, here be the kay of zellar, gie Tim a half a paint more zider ; and thee mai'st have a drap theesell, gall.   Waipe thee mouth fust."

"Ah," said Tim, favouring me with a wink, in the excess of his glory, " rackon they Carnishers 'll know the wai off Tossil's Barton varm next taime, wi'out no saign postesses." *

* Every word of Tim's story is true, except as regards the names.

CHAPTER VI.

Two or three days after this, I was keeping school in the dairy, the parlour being too small for that purpose, and the kitchen and "wash-up" (as they called the back-kitchen) too open to inroads from Suke and Tim. My class consisted of ten, or rather was eight strong, the two weanies (big baby and little baby), only attending for the sake of example, and because they would have roared, if parted from the other children. So those two were allowed to spraddle on the floor, where sometimes they made little rollers of themselves, with much indecorum, and between whiles sat gravely sucking their fat red fingers, and then pointed them in a glistening state at me or my audience, and giggled with a large contempt. The eight, who made believe to learn something, were the six elder Huxtables, and two of Tim Badcock's "young uns." I marshalled them, four on each side, against the low lime-whitened walls, which bore the pans of cream and milk. Little Sally, my head scholar, was very proud of measuring her height, by the horizontal line on the milk-pan where the glazing ended; which Tabitha Badcock, even on tiptoe, could not reach. They were all well "claned," and had white pinnies on, and their ruddy cheeks rubbed up to the highest possible polish, with yellow soap and the jack-towel behind the wash-up door. Hence, I never could relieve them from the idea that Sunday now came every day in the week.

I maintained strict discipline, and allowed no nonsense; but two sad drawbacks constantly perplexed me. In the first place, their ways were so ridiculous, and they laboured so much harder to make me laugh, than they did to learn, that I could not always keep my countenance, and when the spelling-book went up before my face, they knew, as well as possible, what was going on behind it, and peeped round or below, and burst out all together. The second drawback was, that Mrs. Huxtable, in spite of all my protests, would be always rushing in, upon errands purely fictitious; and the farmer himself always found some special business in the yard, close to the wired and unglazed window, whence every now and then his loud haw-haws, and too audible soliloquies, "Dang me! wull done, Zally, that wor a good un; zay un again, cheel! zay un again, wull 'e?" utterly overthrew my most solemn institutions.

" Coom now, smarl chillers"—I addressed them in my unclassical Devonshire dialect, for it kept their attention alive to criticise me when. I "spak unvitty"—" coom now, e've a been spulling lang enough : ston round me now, and tull me what I axes you."

Already, I had made one great mistake, by saying "round" instead of "raound," and Billy, the genius of the family, was upon the giggle.

" Now thun, wutt be a quadripade ? "

" Ai knoo ! " says Sally, with her hand held out.

" Zo do ai," says Jack, thrusting forth his stomach.

" Who wur axing of you ? " I inquire in a stately manner. " You bain't the smarl chillers, be 'e ? Bill knows," I continue, but wax doubtful from the expression of Bill's face.

" Ees fai," cries Bill, suddenly clearing up, " her be wutt moother zits on vor to mulk the coos. Bain't her now ? "

"Thee bee'st ony wan leg out, Bill. Now Tabby Badcock?"

While Tabby is splashing in her memory (for I told them all last week), the farmer much excited, and having no idea what the answer should be, but hoping that one of his own children may discover it first, boldly shows his face at the wired window, but is quite resolved to allow fair play. Not so Mrs. Huxtable, who, in full possession of the case, suddenly appears behind me, and shakes her fist at poor puzzled Tabby. "Thee'dst best pretend to know more than thy betters." She tries to make Tabby hear, without my catching her words. But the farmer hotly shouts, "Lat un alo-un, waife. Tak thee hon from thee mouth, I tull 'e. Spak up now, little wanch."

Thus encouraged, Tabby makes reply, looking crosswise at Mrs. Huxtable.

"Plase, Miss, it be a beastie wi vour taials."

"Raight," cries the farmer, with admiration conquering his disappointment; "raight this taime, ai'll tak my oath on it. I zeed wan to Barnstaple vair last year, and her wor karled, 'Phanominy Quadripade,' her Kirsten name and her zurname, now ai coom to racollack."

Tabby looks elated, and Mrs. Huxtable chagrined. Before I can redress the situation, a sound of heavy blows, delivered on some leathery substance, causes a new stir. All recognise the arrival of Her Majesty's mail, a boy from Martinhoe, who comes upon a donkey twice a week, if there happen to be any letters for the village below.

Out rush Mrs. Huxtable and Suke (who once received an epistle), and the children long to go, but know better. The boy, however, has only a letter for me, which is from Mrs. Shelfer (a cousin of Ann Maples), to whom I wrote a few days since, asking whether she had any rooms to let. Mrs. Shelfer replies that "she has apartments, and they are splendid, and the rent quite trifling;" so the mail is bribed with a pint of cider, while I write to secure a new home.

My departure being now fixed and inevitable, the women naturally began to remonstrate more than ever. It had been settled that Ann Maples should go with me, not to continue as my servant, but to find a place for herself in London.

My few arrangements, which cost me far more pain than trouble, were not long in making; and after saying

good-bye to all the dear little children and weanies, and
kissing their pretty faces in their little beds, amid an
agony of tears from Sally, I was surprised, on entering
the kitchen, to find there Mr. Beany Dawe. There was
little time for talking, and much less for poetry. We
were to start at three in the morning, the farmer having
promised to drive us to meet the coach in Barnstaple,
whence there would be more than thirty miles of hilly
road to Tiverton, the nearest railway station. The
journey to London could thus be made in a day, though
no one in the parish could be brought to believe it.

The poet had been suborned, no doubt, by Mrs.
Huxtable, and now detained me to listen to an elegy
upon the metropolis of England. I cannot stop to
repeat it, neither does it deserve the trouble; but it
began thus :—

"Fayther was wance to Lounon town,
And a zed, zed he, whan a coom down,
' Don't e niver goo there, Ebenezer my son,
For they mulks a coo, when her ain't gat none.
They kapes up sich a hollerin, naight and day,
And a Devonsheer man dunno the impudence they zay.
Their heads and their hats wags regular, like the scratchers of a
        harrow,
And they biles their taties peeled, and ates them in a barrow.

They raides on a waggon top with their wives squazed up inside her,
And they drinks black dose and yesty pops in the place of wholesome
zider.
They wunt take back anything they've zelled,
  And the beds can bite, and the cats can speak :
And a well-dress'd man be a most compelled
  To channge his shirt in the middle of the week ! ' "

" Lor," cried Mrs. Huxtable, " however could they do their washing? Thee vayther must a been as big a liar as thee, Beany. Them gifts always runs in the family."

When, with remarkable patience, I had heard out his elegant effusion, the author, who had conceived much good will towards me, because I listened to his lays and called him Mr. Dawe, the author dived with a deep-drawn sigh into a hole in his sack, and produced in a mysterious manner something wrapped in greasy silver paper, and well tied up. He begged me to accept, and carry it about me most carefully and secretly, as long as I should live. To no other person in the world would he have given this, but I had earned it, as a true lover of poetry, and required it as a castaway among the perils of London. In vain I declined the present; refusal only confirmed his resolution. As the matter

was of so little importance, I soon yielded upon condition that I should first examine the gift. He gave
me leave with much reluctance, and I was surprised at
the beauty and novelty of the thing. It was about the
size of a Geneva watch, but rather thicker, jet black
and shining, and of the exact shape of a human heart.
Around the edge ran a moulding line or cord of
brilliant red, of the same material as the rest. In the
centre was a white spot like a siphuncle. What it was
I could not guess, but it looked like some mineral substance. Where the two lobes met, a small hole had been
drilled to receive a narrow riband. After putting me
through many guesses, Mr. Dawe informed me that it
was a pixie's heart, a charm of unequalled power against
witchcraft and assassination, and to enthral the affection
of a loved one. He only smiled, and rubbed his nose,
on hearing that I should never want it in the last
capacity. Being greatly pleased with it, I asked him
many questions, which he was very loth to answer.
Nevertheless I extorted from him nearly all he knew.

As he was sawing into boards a very large oak-tree,
something fell from the very heart of it almost into his
mouth, for poor Ebenezer was only an undersawyer.

As he could not stop the saw without his partner's concurrence, and did not wish to share his prize, he kicked some sawdust over it until he could stoop to pick it up unobserved. In all his long experience of the woods, he had seen but two of these rare and beautiful things, and now assured me that any sawyer was considered lucky who found only one in the course of his career. The legend on the subject was rather quaint and graceful, and deserves a better garb than he or I can furnish.

> "All in the olden time, there lived
>   A little Pixie king,
>   So lovely and so light of foot
>   That when he danced the ring,
> The moonlight always shifted, to gaze upon his face,
> And the cowslip-bells uplifted, rang time with every pace.
>
>   There came a dozen maidens,
>   Almost as tall as bluebells ;
>   The cowslips hushed their cadence,
>   And bowed before the true belles :
> The maidens shyly glancing, betwixt the cummer darts,
> Espied the monarch dancing, and lost a dozen hearts.
>
>   He was fitted up so neatly,
>   With dewdrops for his crown,
>   And he footed it so featly
>   He never shook them down.
> The maids began advancing, along a lily stem,
> Not to stop the monarch's dancing, but to make him look at them.

The king could not afford them
The proper time to gaze,
But sweetly bowed toward them,
At the turn of every maze :
Till full of pretty faces, and his sandals getting worn,
He was puzzled in his paces, and fell upon a thorn.

The maidens broke the magic ring,
And leaped the cummer dart ;
‘ Alas, our little Pixie king,
The thorn is in his heart ! ’
They laid him in a molehill, and piteously they cried :
Yet this was not the whole ill, for all the maidens died.

Each took a spindled acorn, found
Below a squirrel’s nest,
And set the butt against the ground,
The barb beneath her breast :
So truly she addressed the stroke unto her loving part,
That when the acorn grew an oak, it held her little heart.”

By no means a “ little heart,” it seemed to me, for a fairy to have owned, but as large as it was loving. I assured Mr. Dawe that he was quite untaught in fairy lore, or he never would have confounded fairies with pixies, a different class of society. But he treated my learning with utter contempt, and reasonably enough declared that he who spent all his time in the woods must know more than any books could tell.

He also informed me, that the proper name for the lignified fairy heart, was a "gordit:" but he did not choose to tell me what had become of the other, which was not so large or handsome as this, yet it had saved him a month's sawing, and earned him "a rare time," which meant, I fear, that the proceeds had been spent in a very long cruise.

After refusing all compensation, Mr. Dawe made his farewell in several couplets of uncouth but hearty blessing, begging me only to shake hands with him once, and venturing as a poet to prophesy that we should meet again. The "gordit" was probably nothing more than a rare accretion, or ganglion, in the centre of an aged oak. However, it was very pretty; and of course I observed the condition upon which I had received it, valuing it moreover as a token of true friends.

But how can I think of such trifles, while sitting for the last time in the room where my mother died? To-morrow all the form and colour of my life shall change; even now I feel once more my step on the dark track of justice, which is to me revenge. How long have I been saunter-ing on the dreary moor of listlessness and hollow weariness, which spreads, for so many dead leagues, below the precipice of grief? How long have I been sauntering, not caring to ask where, and conscious of existence only through the nerves and fibres of the memory. The things I have been doing, the duties I have discharged, the vague unlinked ideas, startling me by their buffoonery to grief—might not these have all passed through me, every whit as well, if I had been set against a wall, and wound up for three months, and fitted with the mind expressed in the chuckle of a clock? Nay, worse than all—have I not allowed soft thoughts to steal throughout my heart, the love of children, the warmth of kindness, the pleasure of doing good in however small a way? Much more of this, and I shall learn forgiveness of my wrong!

But now I see a clearer road before me. Returning health renews my gall. Death recedes, and lifts his train from the swords that fell before him. Once more my pulse beats high with hatred, with scorn of meanness, treachery, and lies, with admiration of truth and manhood, not after the fashion of fools.

But dare I mount the Judge's throne? Shall the stir of one frail heart, however fresh from its Maker's hand, be taken for His voice pronouncing right and wrong?

These thoughts give me pause, and I dwell again with my mother. But in all the strength of youth and stern will, I tread them down; and am once more that Clara Vaughan whose life shall right her father's death.

CHAPTER VII.

AT last we got through our parting with the best of people (far worthier than myself to interest any reader), and after it the dark ride over the moors, and the farmer's vain attempt at talking to relieve both himself and us. The honest eyes were bright with tears, tears of pity for my weakness, which now he scarcely cared to hide, but would not show by wiping away ; and how many times he begged for frequent tidings of us, which Sally could now interpret, if written in large round hand. How many times he consulted, commanded, and threatened the coachman, and promised him a goose at Michaelmas, if he took good care of us and our luggage! These great kindnesses, and all the trifling cares which strew the gap of long farewells, were more to think of than to tell. But I ought to mention, that much against the farmer's will, I insisted on paying him half the sum, which he had lent me in a manner never to be forgotten. Moreover, with the same presentiment which he had always felt, he made me promise once more to send for him, if I fell into any dreadful strait.

It was late at night when our cabman, the most polite, and (if his word may be trusted) the most honourable of mankind, rang the bell of Mrs. Shelfer's house. The house was in a by-street near a large unfinished square, in the northern part of London. Mrs. Shelfer came out at once, sharp and quick and short, and wonderfully queer. At first she took no notice at all of either of us, but began pulling with all her strength at the straps of the heaviest boxes, which, by means known to herself alone, she contrived to drag through the narrow passage, and down three low steps into the little kitchen. Then she hurried back, talking all the time to herself, re-opened the door of the fly, jumped in, and felt under both the seats, and round the lining. Finding nothing there, she climbed upon the driver's box, and thoroughly examined both that and the roof. Being satisfied now that none of our chattels were left in the vehicle, she shook her little fist at two or three boys, who stood at the corner near the mews,

and setting both hands to the farmer's great hamper or
" maun " (as he called it), she dragged it inside the front
door, and turned point blanc upon me.

" Pray, my good friend, how many is there ? "

" I'm sure I don't know, Mrs. Shelfer, your cousin
knows best."

" Ah, they're terrible fellows them cabbies, terrible ! "
The cabman stood by all the time, beating his hands
together. " 'Twas only last time I went to Barbican,
one of 'em come up to me, 'Mrs. Shelfer,' says he, 'Mrs.
Shelfer !' says I, 'pray my good friend, how do you
know my name ?' 'Ho, I knows Charley well enough,'
says he, 'and there ain't a better fellow living.' 'A deal
too good for you,' says I, 'and now pray what's your
business with me ?' 'Why, old lady,' he says, as impudent as the man with the wooden leg, 'you've been
and left your second best umbrella under the seat of
the Botany Bay Bus.' 'Catch me !' says I. 'It's Bible
truth,' says he, 'and my old woman's got it now.' 'If
you never get drunk,' says I, 'till that umbrella runs in
your shoes, your old woman needn't steal her lights,'
and with that I ran between the legs of a sheep,
hanging up with my Tuscan bonnet on trimmed with

white—nothing like it, my good friend, the same as I've had these two and twenty years."

"What for, Mrs. Shelfer?" I asked in great surprise.

"Why, for the butcher to see me, to be sure, Miss. You see he wanted to get me down the mews, and murder me with my little wash-leather bag, as I was going to pay the interest on Shelfer's double-barrel gun. Ah yes," with a short sigh, "and there'll be four and ninepence again, next Tuesday."

Talking at this rate, and stopping for no reply, she led us into her kitchen, saying that she would not light a fire upstairs, it was so bootiful, the trimmings of the grate, because she wasn't certain that we would come, but she had got supper for us, excuse me, my good friend, in her own snug little room, and bootiful they was sure enough, the wind last week had made them so fat.

She pointed in triumph to a large dish on the table piled up with blue shells.

"Why, Mrs. Shelfer, they are muscles," I exclaimed with some disgust.

"Ah I see you knows 'em, that they are, Miss, and as bootiful as ever you ate. Charley and me sits down to a peck of them. But the man as comes round with the catsmeat's brother the man with the truck and his eyes crossed, he told me there was such a demand for them in Grosvenor Square, and they was so cunning this weather when they gets fat, he hadn't more than half a peck left, but they was the best of the lot. Now I'll have them all bootiful hot, bootiful, boiling my good friend, if you'll just run upstairs, and a teaspoon and a half of salt, and Cousin Ann knows the way, and the apartments is splendid, splendid, Miss Vaughan!"

She drew herself up, at the end of the sentence, with an air of the greatest dignity; then suddenly dropped it again, and began bustling in and out. Now for the first time, I had leisure to examine her, for while she spoke, the short jumps of her ideas unsettled my observation.

She was a little body, rather thin, with a face not strongly peculiar, but odd enough to second the oddities of her mind. No doubt she had once been pretty, and her expression was pleasant now, especially when a glimpse was afforded of her quick grey eyes, which generally avoided the gaze, and dropped beneath a fringe of close-set lashes. But the loss of the front teeth, and the sharpening and wrinkling of the face, with the straggling neglect of the thick black hair fraying out from the black cap, and the habit she had of shutting her mouth with a snap, all these interfered with her credit for pristine good looks. Like Mrs. Huxtable, she was generally in a bustle, but a bustle of words more often than of deeds. She had no deception about her, yet she never knew the difference between the truth and a lie, and could not understand that any one else should do so. Therefore she suspected everything and everybody, till one of her veins of opinion was touched, and then she would swallow anything.

Tired out with the long day's travel, the dazing of railway speed, and the many scenes and faces which had flashed across me, I could not appreciate the beauty of Mrs. Shelfer's furniture; but leaving Ann Maples to eat the muscles, if she could, and to gossip with her cousin, I was not slow to revisit the old farmhouse, and even the home of my childhood, in the winged cradle of sleep.

CHAPTER VIII.

ANN MAPLES had done her best to persuade me to call on my godmother, Lady Cranberry, but I was quite resolved to do nothing of the sort. In the first place, Lady Cranberry was a person of great wealth, living in a very large house, and keeping up such state as gay widows love, who have forgotten old affections and are looking out for new. In me, therefore, to whose fixed estimate fidelity seemed the very pith of honour, there could be no love towards such a changeling. And even if I had liked her, my circumstances would not admit of our visiting upon equal terms, and it was not likely that I would endure to be patronized by any one. In the second place, the same most amiable lady had written letters of beautiful condolence, and taken a tender interest in our change of fortune, so long as there was any novelty in it; but soon flagged off, and had not even replied to my announcement of dearest mother's death. Finally, I hated her without any compromise, from what I had seen of her, and what she had done to me at Vaughan Park.

So my good Ann set off all alone, for she hoped to obtain some recommendation there, and I was left to receive Mrs. Shelfer's morning visit.

Her queer episodical conversation, and strange biographies of every table, chair, and cushion—her "sticks," as she delighted to call them—I shall not try to repeat, for my history is not a comic one; neither will she appear, unless the connexion requires it. One vein of sympathy between us was opened at once, by her coming into the room with a lame blackbird on her finger; and I was quite surprised at the number of her pets. As for the "splendid apartments," they were two little rooms on the first floor, adjoining one another, and forming, together with the landing outside and a coal-closet, the entirety of that storey. The rooms above were occupied by a young dressmaker. Mr. and Mrs. Shelfer, who had no children kept the ground-floor (consisting of a parlour and kitchen) and the two attics, one of which was always full of onions and carrot seed. Upon the whole, though the "sticks" were very old, and not over clean, until I scoured them, and the drawing-room (as my landlady loved to call it) was low and small, and looked through the rails of a narrow balcony upon a cheese-monger's shop across the road (instead of a wooded dingle), I was very well satisfied with them; and above all the rent was within my means.

In the afternoon, when things were growing tidy, a carriage drove up rapidly, and a violent ringing of the bell ensued. It was Lady Cranberry, who, under the pretext of bringing Ann Maples home, was come to gratify her own sweet curiosity. She ran upstairs in her most charming manner, caught me by both hands, and would have kissed me desperately, if I had shown any tendency that way. Then she stopped to admire me.

"Oh, you lovely creature! How you are grown to be sure! I should never have known you. How delicious all this is!"

Of course I was pleased with her admiration; but only for a moment, because I disliked her.

"I am glad you find it delicious," I replied quite coldly; "perhaps I shall by-and-by."

"What would I give to be entering life under such sweetly romantic circumstances? Dear me! I must introduce you. What a sensation you will cause! With such a face and figure and such a delightful story, we shall all rave about you. And how well you are dressed from that outlandish place! What a piece of luck! It's the greatest marvel on earth that you found me in London now."

"Excuse me," I said, "I neither found, nor meant to find you."

"Oh, of course you are cross with me. I forgot about that. But who made your dress, in the name of all woodland graces?"

"I always make my own dresses."

"Then you shall make mine. Say no more about it. You shall live with me, and make my dresses by day; and by night you shall go with me everywhere, and I won't be jealous. I will introduce you everywhere. 'This is my ward, Miss Vaughan, whose father —ah, I see, you know that romantic occurrence in Gloucestershire.' Do you think it will be a year— and the Great Exhibition season—before you are mistress of a property ten times the size of Vaughan Park?

If you doubt it, look in the glass. Ah me! You know nothing of the world, I forget, I *am* so warm-hearted. But you may take my word for it. Will you cry a bargain?"

She held out her hand, as she had seen the fast men do, whose society she affected. I noticed it not, but led her on; my fury had long been gathering. I almost choked when she spoke in that way of my father, utterly as I despised her. But I made it a trial of self-control, which might be demanded against more worthy objects.

"Are you sure that I shall be useful? Sure that I shall earn my board?"

"Oh, you Vaughans are always so conscientious. I want an eider-down petticoat quilted at once for the winter, and I dare not trust it to Biggs, I know she will pucker it so. That shall be the first little job for my Clara."

Her cup was full. She had used dearest mother's fond appellative, and, as I thought, in mockery. I did not lower myself by any sarcastic language. She would not have understood it. I merely opened the door, and said calmly to my landlady, who was there, of course "promiscuously;" "Mrs. Shelfer, show out the Countess of Cranberry."

Poor godmother, she was so frightened that I was sorry for her. They helped her into the carriage, and she had just strength to draw down the blinds.

Mrs. Shelfer had been in raptures at having so grand a vehicle and two great footmen at her door. Lest the street should lose the effect, she had run in and out a dozen times, and banged the door, and got into talk with the coachman, and sent for beer to the Inn, though she had it in the house. She now came again to my door, in what she called a " terrible quandary." I could not attend to her, but locked myself in, and wrestled with my passionate nature, at one time indulging, then spurning and freezing it. Yet I could . not master it, as I fancied I had done.

CHAPTER IX.

Soon afterwards, Ann Maples went to the place which she had obtained in Lady Cranberry's household; and I determined to begin my search.

"Mrs. Shelfer, do you know London well?"

My landlady was feeding her birds, and I had made up for her disappointment about Lady Cranberry, by fitting the lame blackbird with a wooden leg, cut from a skewer, and tipped with a button: it was pretty to see how kindly and cleverly he took to it, and how proudly he contemplated it, when he thought there was no one watching. His mistress now stopped her work, and made ready for a long speech, with the usual snap of her lips.

"Know London, Miss Vaughan! I was born in Red Cross Street, and I've never been further out of town than Chalk Farm fair, or Hampstead Waterworks, and, please God, I never will. Bless me, what an awful place the country is, awful! What with the trees, and the ditches, and the sting-nettles, and the black wainscot with skewers on the top—"

"Too bad of you, Mrs. Shelfer, to be frightened at palings—and your husband a gardener, too! But tell me whereabouts is Grove Street?"

"What Grove Street, my good friend?"

"Grove Street, London, to be sure."

"Why, dear me, Miss, I thought you knew every-thing; you can doctor Jack, and the Bully, and tell me all about Sandy the squirrel's tail and the hair coming off and when it's going to rain! Don't you know there's a dozen Grove Streets in London, for all I know. Leastways I knows four."

"And where are those four, Mrs. Shelfer?"

"Now please, my good friend, give me just a minute to think. It is dreadful work to be hurried, ever since I fell downstairs, when I were six year old. Let me see now. Charley knows. Can't you wait, Miss, till Charley comes home, and he's coming quite early this evening, and two friends of his to supper."

"No, Mrs. Shelfer, I cannot wait. If you can't tell me, I must go and get a book."

"Oh them books is no good. Why they ain't got
Charley in, and he with the lease one time of the garden
in Hollyhock Square, and a dahlia named after him at
the Royal Heretical Society! And they did say the
Queen would have handed him the spade she liked his
looks so much, only his nails wasn't clean. Very likely
you heard, Miss—And how he was cheated out of it."

"Do you expect me to wait all day?"

"No no, my good friend, to be sure not. You never
will wait a minute, partikler when I spill the coals, and
when I wants to baste the meat. And how can the
gravy run, and a pinch of salt in the dripping-pan—"

"Yesterday, Mrs. Shelfer, you basted my pound and a
half of mutton with three pounds of coals. Now don't
go off into a treatise. Answer me, where is Grove
Street?"

"Bless my heart, Miss Vaughan. You never gives
one a chance. And we thought a young lady from the
country as had been brought up with tags, and lace, and
bobbin, and pigs, and hay—"

"Could be cheated anyhow. No, I don't mean that:
I beg your pardon, dear Patty. I often speak very
hastily. What I mean is that you thought I should

know nothing at all. And I don't know much, but one thing I do know, that you would never cheat me much."

To my surprise she was not at all sensitive on this subject. In fact she had dealt with so many lodgers, that she expected to be suspected. But I believe she never cheated me more than she could help. She answered me quite calmly, after some meditation :

"To be sure, Miss, to be sure, I only does my dooty. A little dripping may be, or a drop of milk for old Tom, and a piece of soap you left in the water, Miss, I kept it for Charley to shave with."

"Now, Mrs. Shelfer, no more of that. Come back to Grove Street; surely, I have given you time enough now."

" Well, Miss, there is one I know close by here. You keep down the Willa Road, and by the fishmonger's shop, and then you turn on the right over against the licensed pursuant to Act of George the Fourth. I knows George the Fourth acted badly, but I never thought it was that way. Sam the Sweep lives with him, and the young man with a hook for his hand that lets out the ' Times ' for a penny, and keeps all his brothers and sisters."

"And where are the other three that you know ? "

" There's one in Hackney, and one in Bethnal Green,

and there's one in Mile-end Road. Bless me, to be sure! I've been there with dear Miss Minto after a cat she lost, a tabby with a silver collar on, and a notch in his left ear. It would make you cry, Miss—"

"Thank you, Mrs. Shelfer; that will do for the present. I'll go up to the 'drawing-room' now."

In a few minutes I went forth with my dark plaid shawl around me, which had saved my mother's life, and was thenceforth sacred. It was the first time I walked all alone in London, and though we lived quite in the suburbs it seemed very odd to me. For a while I felt rather nervous, but no one molested me then or at any other time; although I have heard some *plain* young ladies declare that they could not walk in London without attracting unpleasant attention. Perhaps because they knew not the way either to walk or to dress.

Without any trouble, I found No. 19, Grove Street, then rang the bell and looked round me. It was a clean unpretentious street, not to be known by its architecture from a thousand others in London. The bell was answered by a neat little girl, and I asked for the Master of the house. Clever tactics truly for commencing a task like mine

Being told that the Master was from home, I begged to see the Mistress. The little maid hesitated awhile, with the chain of the door in her hand, and then invited me into the parlour, a small room, but neat and pretty.

"Please, Miss, what name shall I say?"

"Miss Vaughan, if you please." Then I said to myself, "What good am I? Is this my detective adroitness?"

Presently a nice old lady, with snow-white hair, came in.

"Miss Vaughan," she asked with a pleasant smile, "do you wish to see me?"

"Yes, if you please. Just to ask a few questions as to the inmates of this house."

Despite her kindness and good breeding, the lady stared a little.

"May I inquire your motives? Do you know me at all? I have not the pleasure of knowing you."

"My motives I must not tell you. But, as a lady, I assure you, that curiosity is not one. Neither are they improper."

She looked at me in great surprise, examined me closely, and then replied:

"Young lady, I believe what you say. It is impossible not to do so. But my answering you must depend on the nature of your inquiries. You have done, excuse my saying it, you have done a very odd thing."

"I will not ask many questions. How many people live here?"

"I will answer you curtly as you ask, unless you ask what I do not choose to answer. Four people live here, namely, my husband, myself, our only daughter—but for whom I might have been ruder to you—and the child who let you in. Also a woman comes every day to work."

"Are there no more? Forgive my impertinence. No strangers to the family?"

"No lodgers whatever. My son is employed in the City, and sleeps there. My only daughter is in very weak health, and though we do not want all the house, we are not obliged to take lodgers. A thing I never would do, because they always expect to be cheated."

"And is your husband an Englishman?"

"Yes, and an English writer, not altogether unknown."

She mentioned a name of good repute in the world of letters, as even I was aware.

"You have quite satisfied me. I thank you most heartily. Very few would have been so polite and kind. I fear you must think me a very singular being. But I have powerful motive, and am quite a stranger in London."

"My dear, I knew that at once. No Londoner would have learned from me the family history I have told you. I should have shown them out at the very first question. Thank you, oh thank you, my child. But I am sure you have hurt yourself. Oh, the shell has run into your forehead."

As she looked so intently at me, on her way to the door of the room, her foot had been caught by the claw of the what-not, and I barely saved her from falling.

"No, Mrs. Elton, I am not hurt at all. How stupid of me, to be sure. And all my fault that you fell. I hope the shell is not broken. Ah, I bring very bad luck to all who treat me kindly."

"The shell is not worth sixpence. The fault was all my own. If you had not been wonderfully quick, I must have fallen heavily. Pray sit down, and recover yourself, Miss Vaughan. Look, you have dropped a letter. Dear me, I know that writing! Excuse me; it is I that am now impertinent."

"If you know that writing, pray tell me how and where."

The letter she had seen was the anonymous one which brought me from Devonshire to London. I had put it into my pocket, thinking that it might be wanted. It fell out as I leaped forward, and it lay on the floor wide open.

"May I look at the writing more closely? Perhaps I am deceived."

For a while I hesitated. But it seemed so great a point to know who the writer was, that I hushed my hesitation. However, I showed the letter so that she could not gather its import.

"Yes," said Mrs. Elton, "I am quite certain now. That is the writing of a Polish lady, whom at one time I knew well. My husband has written a work upon Poland, which brought him into contact with some of the refugees. Among them was a gentleman of some scientific attainments, who had a pretty lively warm-hearted wife, very fond of dancing, and very fond of dogs. She and I have had many a laugh at one another and ourselves; for, though my hair is grey, I am fond of lively people."

"And where is that lady now?"

"My child, I cannot tell you. Her name I will tell you, if you like, when I have consulted my husband. But it will help you very little towards finding her; for they change their names almost every time they move. Even in London they forget that they are not heard every time they sneeze. The furtive habits born of oppression cling about them still."

"And where did they live at the time you knew them?"

Wrung by suspense and anxiety, I had forgotten good manners. But Mrs. Elton had good feeling which knows when to dispense with them. Nevertheless I blushed with shame at my own effrontery.

"Not very far from here, in a part that is called 'Agar Town.' But they have now left London, and England too, I believe. I must tell you no more, because they had reasons for wishing to be unknown."

"Only tell me one thing. Were they cruel or violent people?"

"The very opposite. Most humane and warm-hearted. They would injure no one, and hated all kinds of cruelty.

How pale you are, my child! You must have a glass of wine. It is useless to say no."

As this clue, which seemed so promising, led to nothing at all, I may as well wind it up at once, and not tangle my story with it. Mr. Elton permitted his wife to tell me all she knew about the Polish exiles, for they were gone to America, and nothing done here could harm them. But at the same time he made me promise not to mention to the police, if my case should ever come before them, the particulars which he gave me; and I am sure he would not wish me to make free with the gentleman's name. A gentleman he was, as both my kind friends assured me, and not likely to conceal any atrocious secret, unless he had learned it in a way which laid it upon his honour. Mr. Elton had never been intimate with him, and knew not who his friends were, but Mrs. Elton had liked the lady who was very kind and passionate. Also she was very apt to make mistakes in English names, and to become confused at moments of excitement. Therefore Mrs. Elton thought that she had confounded the Eltons' address with that of some other person; for it seemed a most unlikely thing that she should know the residents at two

Nos. 19 Grove Street. However so it proved—but of that in its place. It was now six months since they had quitted London, perhaps on account of the climate, for the gentleman had been ill some time, and quite confined to the house. It would be altogether vain to think of tracing them in America. While living in London they owned a most magnificent dog, a truly noble fellow but afflicted with a tumour. This dog suddenly disappeared, and they would not tell what had become of him, but the lady cried most violently one day when he was spoken of. Directly after this they left the country, with a very brief farewell.

All this I learned from Mr. and Mrs. Elton during my second visit, for Mrs. Elton was too good a wife to dispense with her husband's judgment. Also I saw their daughter, a pleasing delicate girl; they learned of course some parts of my story, and were most kind and affectionate to me; and I am proud to have preserved their friendship to the present time. But as they take no prominent share in the drama of my life, henceforth they will not be presented upon its stage.

As I returned up the Villa Road, thinking of all I had heard, and feeling down at heart, something cold was gently placed in my ungloved hand. Turning in surprise and fright I saw an enormous dog, wagging his tail, and looking at me with magnificent brown eyes. Those great brown eyes were begging clearly for the honour of my acquaintance, and that huge muzzle was deposited as a gage of love. As I stooped to ascertain his sentiments, he gravely raised one mighty paw and offered it to me delicately, with a little sigh of self-approval. Upon my accepting it frankly and begging to congratulate him upon his noble appearance and evident moral excellence, he put out his tongue, a brilliant red one, and gave me a serious kiss. Then he shrugged his shoulders and looked with patient contempt at a nicely-dressed young lady, who was exerting her lungs at a silver whistle some fifty yards down the road. "Go, good dog," I said with a smile, "run, that's a good dog, your Mistress wants you immediately." "Let her wait," he said with his eyes, "I am not in a hurry this morning, and she doesn't know what to do with her time. However, if you think it would be rude of me—" And with that he resumed a long bone, laid aside while he chatted to me, tucked it lengthwise in his mouth, like a tobacco-pipe, and after shaking hands again, and saying " Now don't forget me," the great dog trotted away sedately, flourishing his tail on high, like a plume of Pampas grass. At the corner of the railings he overtook his young Mistress, whose features I could not descry ; though from her air and walk I knew that she must be a pretty girl. A good-tempered one too she seemed to be, for she only shook her little whip lightly at the dog, who made an excursion across the road and sniffed at a heap of dust

CHAPTER X.

ALTHOUGH Ann Maples was not so very talkative, it would be romantic to suppose that Mrs. Shelfer had failed to learn my entire history, so far at least as her cousin knew it.

Having now disposed of one Grove Street, I was about to try the same rude tactics with another, viz. that in Hackney; when my landlady gave a little nervous knock, and hurried into the room. " Oh, Miss Vaughan, is it about them willains you are wandering about and taking on so, and frightening all of us nearly to death ?"

" Mrs. Shelfer, I shall feel obliged by your leaving me to manage my own affairs."

" Bless you, Miss, so I will. I wouldn't have them on my mind for the Bank of England, and Guildhall, paved with Lombard Street, and so I told Charley last night. Right, my good friend, quite right, you may depend upon it." Here she tapped her forehead, and looked mysterious.

"That being so, Mrs. Shelfer, I need say nothing more ;" and with that I was going away.

"No, no, to be sure not. Only listen to me, Miss, one minute; and I knows more about willains, a deal more than you do of course, Miss. Why, ever since that rogue who come to Miss Minto's with brandyballs and rabbitskins on a stick."

"Once more, Mrs. Shelfer, I have no time to spare for gossip—"

"Gossip ! No, no, Miss Vaughan ; if you ever heard any one say Patty Shelfer was a 'gossip,' I'll thank you for their name. Gossip ! A mercy on me with all I has to do, and the days drawing in so, and how they does charge for the gas, and the directors holds a meeting first Tuesday in every month, and fills up the pipes with spittle, that's the reason it sputters so, Charley told me."

"Good bye, Mrs. Shelfer."

"No, no. One minute, Miss Vaughan ; you are always in such a hurry. What Charley and me was talking about last night was this. My Uncle John, a

very high class man, first-rate, first-rate, Miss Vaughan,
has been for ever so long in the detective police.
There's nothing he don't know of what goes on in
London, from the rats as comes up the drain pipes to
the Queen getting up on her throne. A wonderful man
he is. I said t'other day—"

"Is he like you, Mrs. Shelfer ?"

"Like me, my good friend ! No, no. And I wouldn't
be like him for something. With all them state secrets
upon him. Why he daren't sneeze out of his hat. But if
you'll only put off going again till to-morrow, he'll be here
this very night about the plate they stole in the Square.
And I'm sure you can't do better than hear what he
thinks about you. He'll be sure to know all that was
done at the time. Bless you, he has got to make all
the returns ; what that is, I don't know. It's a kind of
tobacco Charley says, that they smokes in the Queen's
pipe. But I think it's the convicts as returns from
Botany Bay."

" Well, Mrs. Shelfer, I'll think of what you say, and I
am much obliged to you for the suggestion ; but I can't
bear the idea of coming before the Police again, with a
matter in which they failed so signally."

" But you know, my good friend, it need not be put on the books at all. He'll tell us what he thinks of it, private like, and for the love of the thing."

" If I see him at all, I must beg to see him alone."

" To be sure, my good friend. Quite right, Miss Vaughan, quite right. I'm sure I would rather have the plumber's ladle put to my ear, than one of them horrible secrets."

" Mrs. Shelfer, have I told you any? Now remember, if you ever again allude to this subject before me, I leave your house that day. You ought to know better, Mrs. Shelfer."

" You are quite right, Miss Vaughan ; I ask your pardon, you are quite right. The very words as Charley said to me the other night. 'You ought to have knowed better, Patty, that you did.' "

Away she went, smoothing her apron, patting the fray of her hair—for she never wore side-combs—and mumbling down the stairs. " Quite right, my good friend, quite right, I ought to have knowed better, poor thing."

She brought up my dinner and tea, without a single word, but with many sly glances at me from her quick grey eyes. Once or twice she was at the point of speaking, and the dry smile she always spoke with fluttered upon her face; but she closed her lips firmly and even bit them to keep herself in. I could scarcely help laughing, for I liked the odd little thing; but she was so free with her tongue, that the lesson was sadly wanted.

Late in the evening, she came to say that Inspector Cutting was there, and would come up if I wished it. Upon my request he came, and one look was enough to show that his niece had not misdescribed him. An elderly man, but active looking and wiry, with nothing remarkable in his features, except the clear cast of his forehead and the firm set of his mouth. But the quick intelligence that shot from his eyes made it seem waste of time to finish telling him anything. For this reason, polite though he was, it became unpleasant to talk to him. It was something like shooting at divers—as my father used to describe it—for whom the flash of the gun is enough.

Yet he never once stopped or hurried me, until my tale was done, and all my thoughts laid bare. Then he asked to see all my relics and vestiges of the deed; even my gordit did not escape him.

" L. D. O." he said shortly, " do you speak Italian ?'

" I can read it, but not speak it."

" Is it commoner for Italian surnames to begin with an O, or with a C?"

" There are plenty beginning with both ; but more I should think with a C."

When all my particulars had been told, and all my evidence shown, I asked with breathless interest—for my confidence in him grew fast—what his opinion was.

" Allow me, young lady, to put a few questions to you, on matters you have not mentioned. Forgive me, if they pain you. I believe you feel that they will not be impertinent."

I promised to answer without reserve.

" What was your mother's personal appearance ?"

" Most winning and delicate."

" How old was she at the time of her marriage ?"

" Twenty-one, I believe."

" How old was your father then ?"

" Twenty-five."

" How many years were they married ?"

" Sixteen, exactly."

" When did your guardian first leave England?"

"In the course of a year or two after the marriage."

"Had there been any misunderstanding between him and your father?"

"None, that I ever heard of."

"Did your father, at any time, travel on the continent?"

"Only in Switzerland, and part of Italy, during his wedding tour."

"Your guardian returned, I believe, at intervals to England?" I had never told him this.

"Yes. At least I suppose so, or he would not have been in London."

"Did he visit then at Vaughan Park?"

"Not once within my memory."

"Thank you. I will ask no more. It is a strange story; but I have known several much more strange. Of one thing be assured. I shall catch the criminal. I need not tell you that I heard much of this case at the time."

"Were you sent down to Gloucestershire?"

"No. If I had been—well, I will not say. But I was not then in my present position. Had I been so, it would have become my special department."

"Pray keep me no more in suspense. Tell me what you think."

"That I must not do, or you should know it at once, for my opinion is formed. It would be a breach of duty for me to tell you now."

"Oh," I cried in my disappointment, "I wish I had never seen you."

"Young lady, you have done your duty in placing the matter before me, and some day you will rejoice that you did so. One piece of advice I will give you: change your name immediately, before even the tradesmen about here know it."

"Change my name, Inspector Cutting! Do you think I am ashamed of my name?"

"Certainly not. You have shown great intelligence when a mere child; exert but a little now, and you will see the good sense, or rather the necessity, of my recommendation. When you have gained your object, you may resume your name with pride. You have given your information, Miss Vaughan, as clearly as ever I knew a female give it."

If I detest anything, in the way of small things, it is to be called a "female." So I said coldly; "Inspector

Cutting, I thank you for the compliment. It would be strange indeed if I could not tell with precision, what I have thought of all my life."

"Excuse me, Miss, it would not be strange at all, in a female. And now I will wish you 'good night.' You shall hear from me when needful. Meanwhile, I will take charge of these articles."

He began, in the coolest manner, to pack up my sacred relics, dagger, casts, and all.

"Indeed you won't," I cried, " you shall not have one of them. What are you thinking of?"

He went on with his packing. I saw he was resolute ; so was I. I sprang to the door, locked it, and put the key in my pocket. He said nothing, but smiled.

"Now," I exclaimed in triumph, "you cannot take those away, unless you dare to outrage a young lady."

I was wholly mistaken. He passed by, without touching me, drew some instrument from his waistcoat pocket, and the door stood open before him. All my treasures were in his left hand. I flew at, and snatched them, and then let go with a scream. A gush of blood poured from my hand. He had taken the dagger folded in paper only, and I was cut to the bone. I sank on a chair and fainted.

When I came to myself, Mrs. Shelfer was kneeling before me, with her feet in a basin of water, while two other basins, and numberless towels, were round. Mrs. Shelfer was rubbing my other hand, and crying and talking desperately about her bad luck that day, and a man with eyes crossed whom she had met in the morning. In the background stood Mr. Shelfer himself, whom I had hitherto failed to see, though I believe he had seen me often. He had a pipe in his mouth about a yard long, and seemed wholly undisturbed. "All right, old 'ooman," he said deliberately through his nose, as he saw that I perceived him, "she'll do now, if you don't make too much rumpus." And with that he disappeared, and I had time to pity myself. The hand the poor farmer used so to admire, and which I was proud of no doubt, in my way, lay in a dishcloth covered and oozing with blood. But my relics were on the table, all safe. A quick step was heard on the stairs, and Inspector Cutting came in, carrying a small phial.

"Out of the way, Patty," he cried, "you are doing more harm than good."

He took up a basin of cold water, and poured half the contents of the little phial into it.

"Now hold her arm up, Patty, as high as you can. I never knew arnica fail."

My hand was put into the water, and the bleeding was stanched in a minute or two. However he kept it there for a quarter of an hour, till it was quite benumbed.

"Now you may look at your hand, Miss Vaughan; it will not be disfigured at all. There will be no inflammation. Patty, fetch me some cambric and the best lard; put the young lady to bed at once, and prop her arm up a little."

I looked at my hand, and found three parallel gashes across it, for every edge of the weapon was keen. But only one wound was deep, viz. that across the palm, which was very deep under the thumb. I have the mark of it still. All the wounds were edged with a narrow yellow line.

"Inspector Cutting," I cried, " no power will move me from here, until you promise not to steal my property. Stealing it is, and nothing else. You have no warrant, and my information to you was wholly unofficial."

The last word seemed to move him. They all like big words, however clear-headed they are.

"Miss Vaughan, under these special circumstances, I will promise what you require; upon condition that you give me accurate drawings, for I see that you can make them."

"Certainly, when my hand is well enough."

"Believe me, I am deeply concerned at what has occurred. But the fault was all your own. How dare you obstruct the Police? But I wish some of my fellows had only half your spirit. A little more experience, and nothing will escape you. Come, Miss Vaughan, though you are a lady, or rather because you are one, give me your left hand, in token that you forgive me."

I did so with all my heart. I liked him much better since I had defeated him; and I saw that it was well worth the pain, for he would do his utmost to make amends. He wished me good night with a most respectful bow. "I will come and inquire how you are to-morrow, Miss Vaughan. Patty, quiet, and coolness, and change the lard frequently. No doctor, if you please; and above all hold your queer little tongue."

"Never fear me, Uncle John; you are right, my good

friend, it is a little tongue, but no queerer than my neighbours."

Inspector Cutting would have formed a far lower opinion of my spirit, if he had seen how I cried that night; not from the pain of the wounds, I am sure, but to think of the fuss dear mother would have made about them.

CHAPTER XI.

IN spite of the arnica, my cuts were not healed for a month ; not enough, I mean, for me to handle a pencil. Mr. Cutting, when he came, according to promise, told me something to quiet me, because I was so feverish. Whether he believed it, or only acted medically, was more than I could decide. The opinion he gave me, or the substance of it, was this.

That the deed was done, not for money, or worldly advantage in any way, but for revenge. Here I thought of Mrs. Daldy. What wrong the revenge was wreaked for, he could not even guess, or at any rate would not hint to me.

That the straightest clue to the mystery was to be sought in Italy, where my guardian's track should be followed carefully. The idea of forcing, or worming, the truth from him was rejected at once through my description of his character ; although the Inspector quite agreed with me, that, even if guiltless of the crime, Mr. Edgar Vaughan knew all about it now.

That no importance should be attached to the anonymous letter from London ; in accordance with my promise to Mrs. Elton, I did not mention the Polish lady's name ; and Mr. Cutting did not press me to do so, for he firmly believed from what I said that she had made a mistake in the address she gave, and would not help us now, even if we could find her.   That nevertheless a strict watch should be kept in London, whither flock nine-tenths of the foreigners who ever set foot in this country.   London moreover was likely, ere long, to draw nearly all the migratory strangers to the business or pleasure of next year's " Great Exhibition," provided only that it should prove successful, as the Inspector thought it would.

As for my enemy being attracted by works of industry, it seemed to me quite against nature that a base assassin should care for art or science, or any national progress. But the remembrance of several cases, among the dark annals I used to delight in, soon proved to me my error ; while the long experience of a man, versed from his youth in criminal ways, convicted me of presumption.

To put myself more on a level with fraud, and stealth, and mystery, I did a thing for which I felt guilty to myself and my mother. I changed my name. But, in spite of Inspector Cutting, I did not travel out of the family. My father's second name was "Valentine," taken from his mother. This name I assumed in a shorter form, becoming "Clara Valence;" it saved change of initials and a world of trouble, and I felt warmer in it, because it seemed to have been my father's. In the neighbourhood I knew no one except Mrs. Elton, to whom (as I grew intimate with her) I partly explained my reasons. As for Mrs. Shelfer, she was delighted at the change. She said that her Uncle John had christened me, that it sounded much prettier, and would always remind her of Valentines. Nevertheless I longed for the day when I might call myself "Clara Vaughan" once more.

By the time I was able to go about freely again and use my hand as of old, it was the middle of November. The first use I made of my pencil was to copy most carefully all that Inspector Cutting required. He promised to keep these drawings, and indeed the whole matter, most jealously to himself; by which term he meant, as I afterwards found, Inspector Cutting and those to whom he was bound to report.

What I now wanted was money, to send an adroit inquirer throughout the North of Italy, and other parts where my guardian's shifting abode had been. I knew that he dwelt awhile at Pisa, Genoa, and Milan, also at an obscure little village named " Calva," which I could not find in the maps. All I had learned of his rovings was from the lessons my father would give me sometimes, when he used to say, " Now, Tooty, put your finger on Uncle Edgar." To every one, but myself, it seemed a strange thing that after so many wanderings, Mr. Edgar Vaughan had brought no valet, major domo, or courier, no dependant or retainer of any kind, and not even a foreign friend to England, or at any rate to Vaughan Park.

But now for the needful resources—the only chance of procuring them lay in my young and partly self-tutored art. I braced myself with the remembrance, that while none of my family ever laid claim to genius, the limner's faculty had never been wanting among them. Inferior gifts are often as heirlooms in the blood, though high original power follows no vein except its own. The latter none of us ever possessed ; but taste and the knack of adaptation had seldom been alienated. Observation too, in a small way, and the love of nature seemed inborn in us all. My father's drawings were perfect, but for the one thing wanted; and in sketches from outdoor nature that want was less perceived. My grandfather had been known among the few amateurs of the day as a skilful colourist. As to habits of observation, a little tale handed down in our family will show that they had existed in one of its members seven generations ago.

In the autumn of 1651, when King Charles was stealing along from Colonel Wyndham's house to the coast of Hampshire and Sussex, the little band was overtaken by nightfall, somewhere near the New Forest. It was shortly after the narrow escape of the King from that observant blacksmith, who saw that his horse was shod with North-country iron. Though he was taking it easily, his three trusty friends knew well that a Roundhead Squadron was near, and that his last chance depended on speed and night travel. What could they do now in the tempestuous darkness? They were in a tract thinly inhabited, half woodland, half heather, and the road was hopelessly lost. No rain fell as yet it was true, and the wind was waiting for rain, but the lightning came fitfully from the horizon all round. The King alone was on horseback, his three companions afoot. They stood still in doubt and terror, for they could not tell north from south. Suddenly Major Cecil Vaughan espied a faint gleam familiar to him of old in the waste land round Vaughan Park. To an accurate eye there could be little doubt as to the source of the lambent light—flame it could not be called. It played in a pale yet constant stream on a certain kind of moss, known to botanists, not to me, for the waste lands have been re-claimed. This light is to be seen at no time, except when the air is surcharged with electricity.

"Follow me all; I know the way!" cried Major Vaughan, right cheerily.

"And if you do, man," said the King, "your eyes are made of clashers."

[What this meant, I used as a child to wonder; but now I know.]

For six dark miles the Major led them without default, until they came to a lonely heathman's house, where they slept in safety. He never told them how he did it; being apt, I suppose, as men of the second order are, to hug superior knowledge. But it was a most simple thing. That strangely sensitive moss follows the course of the sun, and therefore the lambent light can only be seen from the west. So all the time he could see it—the others never saw it at all—he knew that they were wending from west to east, which was their proper course.

To return to myself. I put the finishing touch to a view of rock and woodland scenery, north-west of Tossil's Barton, and set off to try my fortune with it. Some young ladies, born to my position, would have thought this errand one of much degradation, but it did not appear so to me. So I walked briskly—for I hate an omnibus, and could ill afford a cab—to the shop of a well-known dealer in pictures, not far from the Hay-market. It was my first venture into the heart of London, but I found the way very easily, having jotted it down from a map. The day was dark and drizzly; the pavement grimy and slimy, and hillocked with mud at the joints of the flags. It was like walking on a peeled kneading-trough with dollops of paste left in it. Along the far reach of the streets, and the gardens in the squares, wisps of fog were crawling, and almost every one was coughing.

The dealer received me politely. Too politely in fact: for it seemed to savour of kindness, which I did not want from him. What I wanted was business, and nothing else. He took my poor drawing, done only in water-colours, and set it up in a square place made perhaps for the purpose, where the brown flaw fell upon it from a skylight formed like a Devonshire chimney. Then he drew back and clasped his hands, then shaded his eyes with them, as if the light were too strong, whereas the whole place was like a well turned upside down. He seemed uneasy because I did not care to follow him throughout all this little performance.

"And now," I said, for my foolish pride was up, and I spoke as I would have done to the porter at our lodge, not with the least contempt—I was never so low as that—but with a long perspective, "Now, Mr. Oxgall, it will soon be dark. What will you give me for it?"

"Allow me, Miss; allow me one moment. The light is a leetle too strong. Ah, the mark of the brush comes out. Strong touch, but indiscreet. A year of study required. Shade too broad and massive. A want of tone in the background. Great feeling of nature, but inexperienced rendering. More mellowness desiderated. Full however of promise. All the faults on the right side. Most energetic handling; no weak stippling here. But water-colours are down just now; a deal depends on the weather and time of year."

" How so, Mr. Oxgall ?"

" Hot sun, and off they go. Fog and murk and frost, and the cry is all for oil. Excuse me, Miss—a thousand pardons, your name escaped me, you did not pronounce it strongly."

" Miss Valence !" I said, with an emphasis that startled him out of his mincing.

" Miss Valence, you think me very long. All young ladies do. But my object is to do them justice, and if they show any power, to encourage them."

" Thank you, I want no encouragement. I know I can draw a little ; and there it is. The fog is thickening. I have far to go. Your price, if you please ? "

I went up many steps in his opinion, by reason of my curtness and independence.

" Miss Valence, I will give you three guineas, although no doubt I shall be a loser."

" Then don't give it," said I in pure simplicity.

I went up several steps more. How utterly men of the world are puzzled by plain truth !

"Miss Valence, if you will forgive the observation, I would beg to remark that your conversation as well as your painting is crisp. I will take this little piece at all hazards, because it is full of character. Will you forgive me for one word of advice ?"

"There is nothing to forgive. I shall thank you heartily for it."

"It is simply this :—The worst part of your work is the perspective. And figure-drawing will be of service to you. Study at a school of design, if you have one near you ; and be not above drawing stiff and unsightly objects. Houses are the true guides to perspective. I cannot paint or even draw; but I am so much with great artists, that I know well how to advise."

"Thank you. Can you kindly suggest anything more ?"

"Yes. Your touch is here and there too harsh. Keep your hand light though bold, and your brush just a leetle wetter. But you have the grand things quite unattainable, when not in the grain. I mean, of course, freedom of handling and an artist's eye."

"Do you think I could do any good in oils?"

"I have no doubt you could, but not for a long time. If fame is your object, take to oils. If speedy returns, stick to water-colours. Leave me your address, if you have no objection; and bring me your next work. If I do well with this, I will try to give you more."

He took from a desk three new sovereigns and three new shillings, wrapped them neatly in silver paper, and handed them to me. I never imagined I could be so proud of money.

Light of heart I left the shop, not that I had made my fortune yet, but what was greater happiness, I thought myself likely to make it.

Soon I perceived, with some alarm, how thick and murky the air had grown. The fog was stooping heavily down, and was now become like a wash of gamboge and lamp-black. All the street-lamps were lit, though they could not see one another, and every shop-keeper had his little jet. The pavement was no longer slippery, but sticky and dry; and a cold, that pierced to the bones, was stealing along. Already it had begun to freeze; and I, so familiar both with white and black frost, observed with no small interest the grey or fog-frost, which was new to me. How different from the pure whiteness when the stars are sparkling, and the earth is gleaming, and the spirit of man so buoyant! This grey fog-frost is rather depressing to most natures, and a chilly damp creeps to the core of all things. Thick encrusting rime comes with it, and sometimes a freezing rain.

Before I reached the New Road, the fog had grown so dense and dark, that I was much inclined to take a cab, for fear of losing my way. But I could not see one, and finding myself at last in a main thoroughfare called the Hampstead Road, I walked on briskly and bravely till I reached Camden Town, when I knew what course to pursue.

Slowly wending up College Street, for I was getting tired and the fog thicker than ever, indeed every step seemed a thrust into an ochred wall, I heard a plaintive, and rather musical, voice chanting, much as follows :—

" Christian friends, and sisters in the Lord, all who own a heart that feels for undeserved distress, aid, I implore you, a bereaved wife and mother, who has this very moment seven small lovely children, starving in a garret, three of them upon a bed of sickness, and the

inhuman landlord, for the sake of a few shillings about
to turn them this bitter night into the flinty streets.
Christian friends, may you never know what it is to be
famished as I and my seven darlings are this very night,
in the midst of plenty. From Plymouth in Devonshire,
I walked two hundred and fifty miles afoot all the
way to join my beloved husband in London. When I
came to this Christian city—Georgiana, pick up that
halfpenny—he had been ordered off in the transport
ship Hippopotamus, to shed his blood for his Queen and
country ; and I who have known the smiles of plenty in
my happy rustic home, I am compelled for the sake of
my children to the degradation of publicly soliciting
alms. The smallest trifle, even an old pair of shoes
or a left off garment will be received with the heartfelt
gratitude of the widow and orphan. My eldest child,
ma'am, the oldest of seven, bad in the whooping cough.
Georgiana, curtsey to the pretty lady, and show her
your broken chilblains."

" No thank you," I said : I could just see her through
the fog. She looked like one who had seen better days,
and the thought of my own vicissitudes opened my heart
towards her. How could I show my gratitude better

for the money I had just earned, than by bestowing a share in charity upon worthy objects? So I took out my purse, an elegant little French one given me by dear mother, and placed my three new shillings in the poor creature's hand, as she stood in the gutter. She was overpowered with gratitude, and could not speak for a moment. Then she came nearer, to bless me.

"Sweet lady, in the name of seven famishing innocents, whom you have saved from death this night, may He who guards the fatherless and the widow from His mercy-seat above, may He shower his richest blessings—"

Snap—she had got my purse and was out of sight in the fog. Georgiana's red heels were the last thing I saw. For an instant I could not believe it; but thought that the fog had affected my sight. Then I darted across the road, almost under the feet of a horse, and down a place called "Pratt Street." It was hopeless, utterly hopeless; and not only my three pounds were gone, but half besides of all I had in the world. I had taken that money with me, because I meant, if fortunate with my landscape, to buy a large box of colours in Rathbone-place; but the fog had deterred me. She had snatched my purse while I tried to clasp it, for my glove had first got in the way. All was gone, dear mother's gift, my first earnings, and all. More than all I felt sore at heart from the baseness of the robbery. Nothing is so bitterly grievous to youth as a blow to faith in one's species.

I am not ashamed to confess that feeling all alone in the fog, I leaned against some iron railings and cried away like a child. Child I was still at heart, despite all my trials and spirit; and more so perhaps than girls who have played out their childhood. In the full flow of my passion, for I was actually sobbing aloud, ashamed of myself all the while, I felt an arm steal round my waist, and starting in fear of another thief, confronted the loveliest face that human eyes ever looked on. With soft caresses, and sweetest smiles, it drew close to my own stormy and bitter countenance.

"Are you better now, dear? Oh don't cry so. You'll break your poor little heart. Do tell me what it is, that's a dear. I'll do anything to help you."

"You can't help me:" I exclaimed through my sobs: "Nobody can help me! I was born to ill luck, and shall have nothing else till I die."

"Don't say so dear, You mustn't think of it. My

father, who never is wrong, says there's no such thing as luck."

"I know that well enough. People always say that who have it on their side."

"Ah, I never thought of that. But I hope you are wrong. But tell me, dear, what is the matter with you. I'm sure you have done no harm, and dear papa says no one can be unhappy who has not injured any one."

"Can't they though? Your papa is a moralist. Now I'll just tell you facts." And to prove my point, I told her of this new trouble, hinted at previous ones and my many great losses, of which money was the least. Even without the controversial spirit, I must have told her all. There was no denying anything to such a winning loving face.

"Dear me!" she cried very thoughtfully, with her mites of hands out of her muff—she had the prettiest set of fur I ever beheld, and how it became her!— "Dear me! she couldn't have meant it, I feel quite sure she couldn't. You'll come to my opinion when you have time to consider, dear"—this was said so sagely that I could have kissed her all over like a duck of a baby. "To steal from you who had just given her more than you could afford! Now come with me, dear, you shall have all the money I have got; though I don't think it's anything like the nine pounds you have lost, and I'm sure it is not new money. Only I haven't got it with me. I never carry money. Do you know why, dear?"

"No. How should I?"

"Well, I don't mind telling [you. Because then I can't spend it, or give it away. I don't care a bit about money. What good is it to me? Why, I can never keep it, somehow or other. But papa says if I can show five pounds on Christmas-day, he will put five more on the top of it, and then do you know what I'll do? I'll give away five, and spend the rest for Pappy and Conrad." And the lively little thing clapped her hands at the prospect, quite forgetting that she had just offered me all her store. Presently this occurred to her.

"No. Now I come to think of it, I won't have the five pounds on Christmas-day. As the girls at the College say, I'll just sell the old Pappy. That will be better fun still. He will find a good reason for it. He always does for everything. You shall have every bit of it. Come home with me now, that's a dear. You are better now, you know. Come, that's a love. I am sure I shall love you with all my heart, and you are so terribly unlucky."

I yielded at once. She was so loving and natural, I could not resist her. She broke upon me like soft sunshine through the fog, laughing, smiling, dancing, her face all light and warmth, yet not a shallow light, but one that played up from the fount of tears. Her deep rich violet eyes seldom used their dark lashes, except when she was asleep. She was life itself, quick, playful, loving life, feeling for and with all life around ; pitying, trusting, admiring all things ; yet true as the hearth to household ties. I never found another such nature : it was the perfection of maiden womanhood, even in its unreason. And therefore nobody could resist her. With me, of ten times her strength of will, and power of mind —small though it be—she could do in a moment exactly as she liked ; I mean of course in trivial matters. It was impossible to be offended with her.

When she had led me a few steps towards her home —for I went with her (not, of course, to take her money, but to see her safe), she turned round suddenly :—

" Oh I forgot, dear; I must not take you to our house. We have had new orders. But where do you live ? I will bring you my little bag to-morrow. They won't let me out again to-night. Now I know you will oblige me. I am so sorry that I mustn't see you safe home, dear." This she said with the finest air of protection imaginable.

I gave her my name and address, and asked for hers.

" My name is Isola Ross, I am seventeen and a half, and my papa is Professor at the College. I ran away from old Cora. It seemed such fun to be all alone in the fog. What trouble I shall get into ! But they can't be angry with me long. Kiss me, darling. Mind, to-morrow ! "

Off she danced through the fog ; and I went sadly home, yet thinking more of her, than of my serious and vexatious loss.

CHAPTER XII.

INSPECTOR CUTTING, upon the first tidings of the robbery, came at once, and assured me that he knew the "party" well, and wanted her for several other plants, and crafty as she was ("leary" was the elegant word he used) he was sure to be down upon her in the course of a very short time.

Isola Ross, to my great surprise, did not come the next day, nor even the day after; so I set out to look for her, at the same time wondering at myself for doing so. Knowing that College Street must take its name from some academic building in or near it, I concluded of course that there I should find Professor Ross and my lovely new friend. So without consulting Mrs. Shelfer, who would have chattered for an hour, away I went one fine frosty morning to ask about the College.

I found that a low unsightly building, which I had often passed, near the bottom of the street, was the only

College there; so I entered a small quadrangle, to make further inquiries.

The first person I saw was a young man dressed like one of my father's grooms, and cracking a long whip and whistling. He had a brilliant scarlet neckcloth, green sporting coat, and black boots up to his knees. I studied him for a moment because it struck me that he would look well in a foreground, when toned down a little, as water colours would render him. He appreciated my attention, and seemed proud of it.

"Now, Polly, what can I do for you, dear?"

He must have been three parts drunk, or he would never have dared to address me so. Of course I made no answer, but walked on. He cracked his whip like a pistol, to startle me.

"Splendid filly," I heard him mutter, "but cussed high action." What he meant I do not know or care.

The next I met was a fussy little man, dressed all in brown, who smelt of musty hay.

"Will you kindly tell me," I asked, "where to find Professor Ross?"

"Ross, Ross! Don't know the name. No Ross about here. What's he Professor of?"

"That I was not told. But it is something the young
ladies study."

"No young ladies about here. But I see you have
brought your dear mamma's lapdog. Take it out of the
bag. Let me look at it."

"Is not this the College?"

"Yes to be sure. The best College in London. Quick,
let me see the dog."

"I have no dog, sir. I have made some mistake."

"Then you have got a pony. Pet over-fed. Shetland
breed."

"No indeed. Nothing except myself; and I am
looking for Miss Ross."

"Young lady, you have made a very great mistake.
You have kept me five minutes from a lecture on the
navicular disease. And my practice is controverted by
an upstart youth from the country. I am in search of
authorities." And off he darted, I suppose to the library.

It was clear that I had made some mistake, so I
found my way back to the street, and asked in the
nearest shop what building it was that I had just left.

"Oh, them's the weterans," said the woman, "and a
precious set they be!"

"Why, they did not look like soldiers."

"No, no, Miss. Weterans, where they takes in all the sick horses and dogs. And very clever they are, I have heard say."

"And where is the College where the young ladies are?"

"I don't know of no other College nearer than High Street, where the boys wear flat caps. But there's a girls' school down the road."

"I don't want a school. I want a College where young ladies go."

"Then I cant help you, Miss." And back I went to consult Mrs. Shelfer.

"Bless my soul, Miss Valence," cried the little woman, out of breath with amazement, "have you been among them niggers? It's a mercy they didn't skin and stuff you. What do you think now they did to my old Tom?'

"How can I guess, Mrs. Shelfer?"

"No, no, to be sure not. I forgot, my good friend. Why, they knowed him well it seems, because he had been there in dear Miss Minto's time, for a salmon bone that had got crossways in his œsop, so they said at least, but they are the biggest liars—so only a year ago come next Boxing-day, here comes to the door half a dozen of them, bus-cad and coachman all in one, all looking as grave as judges. When I went to the door they all pulled their hats off, as if I had been the Queen at the very least. 'What can I do for you, my good friends?' says I; for Shelfer was out of the way, and catch me letting them in for all their politeness. No, no, thank you. 'Mrs. Shelfer,' says the biggest of them, a lantern-jawed young fellow with covers over his pockets, 'Mrs. Shelfer, you are possessed of a most remarkable cat. An animal, ma'am, of un-paralleled cemetery and organic dewelopment. Our Professor, ma'am, is delivering a course of lectures on the Canonical Heapatightness of the Hirumbillycuss.'"

"Well done, Mrs. Shelfer! What a memory you must have!"

"Pretty well, Miss, pretty well. Particular for long words, when I likes the sound of them. 'Well sir,' I says, feeling rather taken aback, 'thank God I haven't got it.' 'No, ma'am,' says he, 'your blooming coun-tenance entirely negatives any such dyingnoses. But the Professor, in passing the other morning, observed some symptoms of it in your magnificent cat, for whom he entertains the most sincere attachment, and whom he will cure for our advancement and edification upon the lecture table. And now, ma'am, Professor Sallenders desires his most respectful compliments, and will you allow us to take that dear good cat to be cured. The Professor was instrumental once in preserving his honoured existence, therefore he feels assured that you will not now refuse him.' Well you see, Miss, I didn't half like to let him go, but I was afraid to offend the Professor, because of all my animals, for I knew that he could put a blight upon them, birds and all, if he chose. Old Tom was lying roasting his back again the fender, the same as you see him now, poor soul; so I catched him up and put him in a double covered basket, with a bit of flannel over him, because the weather was cold; and he was so clever, would you believe it, he put up his old paws to fight me, he knew he was going to mischief, and that turned me rather. 'Now will you promise to bring him back safe?' I says. 'Ma'am,' says the lantern-jawed young man, bowing over his heart, and as serious as a pulpit, 'Ma'am, in less than an hour. Rely upon the honour of a Weteran Arian Gent.'"

"Well, Mrs. Shelfer, I am astonished. Even I should

never have been so silly. Poor old Tom among the Philistines!"

"Well, Miss, I began to feel very uneasy directly they was gone. I thought they looked back so queerly, and old Tom was mewing so dreadful in the basket. Presently I began to hear a mewing out of the cupboard, and a mewing out of the clock, and even out of the dripping-pan. So I put on my bonnet as quick as I could, and ran right away to the College, and somehow or other by the time I got there, I was in a fright all over. As good luck would have it, the man was at the gate; a nice respectable married man, and a friend of Charley's. 'Curbs,' I says, 'where is Professor Sallenders?' 'Down in the country,' says he, 'since last Friday. He never stops here at Christmas, Mrs. Shelfer, he's a deal too knowing for that.' My heart went pop, Miss, like an oyster shell in the fire. I held on by the door, and I thought it was all up with me. 'Don't take on so, Missus,' says Curbs, 'if any of your museum is ill, there's half a dozen clever young coves in the operating room over there, only they're busy just now, cutting up a big black cat. My eyes, how he did squeal!' I screamed out and ran—Curbs thought I was mad, and he was not far out—bang went the door before me, and there on the table, with the lantern-jawed young man flourishing a big knife over him, there lay my precious old Tom strapped down on his back, with his mouth tied up in white tape, and leather gloves over his feet, and sticks trussed across him the same as a roasting rabbit, and a streak of white all along his blessed stomach—you know, Miss, he hadn't got one white hair by rights—where the niggers had shaved and floured him, to see what they were about. He turned up his dear old eyes when he saw me; it would have made you cry, and he tried to speak. Oh you precious old soul, didn't I scatter them right and left? I scratched that lantern-jawed hypocrite's face till I gave him the hirumbillycuss and hirumtommycuss too, I expect. I called a policeman in, and there wasn't one of them finished his Christmas in London. But the poor old soul has never been the same cat since. The anxiety he was in, turned his hair white on both sides of his heart and all round the backs of his ears. He wouldn't come to the door, he shook so, at the call of the cat's-meat man for better than a month, and he won't look at it now, while there's a skewer in it."

The poor little woman was crying with pity and rage. Old Tom looked up all the time as if he knew all she said, and then jumped on her lap, and showed his paws, and purred.

Meanwhile, a change had come over my intentions. Perhaps all the rudeness I had met with that day had called my pride into arms. At any rate, much as I liked pretty Isola, and much as I longed for her fresh warm kindness, I now resolved to wait until she should choose to seek me. So I did not even ask Mrs. Shelfer whether she knew the College where the Professor lectured. What were love and warm young hearts to me? I deserved such a rebuff for swerving so from my duty. Now I would give all my thoughts to the art, whence only could spring any hope of attaining my end, and the very next day I would follow the picture-dealer's advice.

CHAPTER XIII.

THERE was a school of design not very far from my lodgings, and thither I went the next morning. My landlady offered to come with me and see me safe in the room; and of course her Charley, who seemed to know everybody, knew some one even there, to whom she kindly promised to recommend me. So I gladly accepted her offer.

In some respects, Mr. Shelfer was more remarkable than even his wife. He was so shy, that on the rare occasions when we met, I never could get him to look at me, except once when he was drunk; yet by some mysterious process he seemed to know everything about me—the colour of my eyes, the arrangement of my hair, the dresses I put on, the spirits I was in—a great deal more, in fact, than I ever cared to know. So that sometimes my self-knowledge was largely increased, through his observations repeated by his wife. But I was not allowed to flatter myself that this resulted from any especial interest; for he seemed to possess an equal acquaintance with the affairs of all his neighbours. Mention any one anywhere around, and he, without seeming to mean it, would describe him or her unmistakably in half a dozen words. He never praised or blamed, he simply identified. He must have seen more with a blink of his eye, than most people see in five minutes of gazing. He seldom brought any one home with him, though he often promised to do so; he never seemed to indulge in gossip, at any rate not with his wife. "Cut it short, old 'ooman," was all the encouragement he ever gave her in that way. When he was at home—a thing of rare occurrence—he sat with his head down and a long pipe in his mouth; he walked in the street with his head down, and never accosted any one. Where did he get all his knowledge? I doubt if there were a public-house in London, but what Shelfer knew at the furthest a cousin of the landlord, and a brother of one of the potboys. "Charley Shelfer" everybody called him, and everybody spoke of him, not with distinguished respect, but with a kindly feeling. His luck was proverbial; he had a room full of things which he had won at raffles, and he was in constant requisition to throw for less fortunate people. As for his occupation—he called himself a nurseryman, but he had no nursery that I could discover. He received a pound a week for looking after the garden in the great square; but when any one came for him, he was never to be found there. I think he spent most of his time in jobbing about, and "swopping" (as Mrs. Shelfer called it) among his brother gardeners. Sometimes, he brought home beautiful plants, perfectly lovely flowers, unknown to me even by name, and many of these he presented to me by Mrs. Shelfer's hands. Every Sunday morning he was up before the daylight, and away for an excursion, or rather an incursion, through the Hampstead, Highgate, and Holloway district. From these raids he used to return as I came home from the morning service. By the way, if I had wanted to puzzle him and find a blank in his universal acquaintance, the best chance would have been to ask him about the clergyman. He never gave the pew-openers any trouble, neither indeed did Mrs. Shelfer, who called herself a Catholic; but the lively little woman's chiefest terror was death, and a parson to her was always an undertaker. If Mr. Shelfer had not spent the Sunday morning quite so well as I had, at any rate he had not wasted his time. I think he must have robbed hen-roosts and allotment grounds; and yet he was too respectable for that. But whence and how could he ever have come by the gipsey collection he always produced from his hat, from his countless pockets, from his red cotton handkerchief, every Sunday at 1 P.M. ? Eggs, chickens, mushrooms, sticks of horseradish and celery, misletoe-thrushes, cucumbers, cabbages red and white, rabbits, watercress, Aylesbury ducks—I cannot remember one quarter of his manifold forage. All I can say is, that if these things are to be found by the side of the road near London, Middlesex is a far better field for the student of natural history than Gloucestershire, or even beloved Devon. Mrs. Shelfer said it was all his luck; but I hardly think it could have rained Aylesbury ducks, even for Mr. Shelfer.

All the time he was extracting from his recesses this multifarious store, he never once smiled, or showed any symptoms of triumph, but gravely went through the whole, as if a simple duty.

How was it such a man had not made his fortune?

Because he had an incurable habit of " backing bills "
for any one who asked him ; and hence he was always
in trouble.

Mrs. Shelfer and I were admitted readily into the
school of design. It was a long low room, very badly
lighted, and fitted up for the time until a better could
be provided. It looked very cold and comfortless ;
forms instead of chairs, and desks like a parish school.
The whitewashed walls were hung with diagrams,
sections, tracings, reductions, most of them stiff and
ugly, but no doubt instructive. At one end was a
raised platform, reserved for lecturers and the higher
powers. Shelves round the wall were filled with casts
and models, and books of instruction were to be had out
of cupboards. Of course we were expected to bring
our own materials, and a code of rules was exhibited.
The more advanced students were permitted to tender
any work of their own which might be of service to
the neophytes. From no one there did I ever receive
any insolence. At first, the young artists used to look
at me rather hard, but my reserved and distant air was
quite enough to discourage them.

After the introduction, which Mrs. Shelfer accomplished in very great style, I dismissed her, and set to in earnest to pore once more over the rudiments of perspective. One simple truth as to the vanishing point struck me at once. I was amazed that I had never perceived it before. It was not set forth in the book I was studying; but it was the sole key to all my errors of distance. At once I closed the book; upon that one subject I wanted no more instruction, I had caught the focus of truth. Books, like bad glass, would only refract my perception. All I wanted now was practice and adaptation of the eye.

Strange as it seemed to me then, I could draw no more that day. I was so overcome at first sight by the simple beauty of truth, mathematical yet poetical truth, that error and obscurity (for there is a balance in all things) had their revenge for a while on my brain. But the truth, once seen, could never be lost again. Thenceforth there were few higher penances for me, in a small way, than to look at one of my early drawings.

When my brain was clear, I returned to do a real day's work. For the cups, and vases, and plates, and things of "aesthetic art" (as they chose to call it), I did not care at all; but the copies and models and figures were most useful to me. Unless I am much mistaken, I made more advance in a fortnight there, than I had in any year of my life before.

With my usual perseverance—if I have no other virtue, I have that—I worked away to correct my many shortcomings ; not even indulging (much as I wanted the money) in any attempts at a finished drawing, until I felt sure that all my foundations were thoroughly laid and set. "And now," I cried towards Christmas, "now for Mr. Oxgall; if I don't astonish him this time, my name is not Clara Vaughan !" It did me good when I was alone, to call myself by my own name, and hug my right to be my father's daughter.

CHAPTER XIV.

MEANWHILE old Christmas was come, and all I was worth in the world was change for half a sovereign. True, my lodgings were paid for, a fortnight in advance, because good Mrs. Shelfer wanted to treat all her pets to a Christmas dinner; but as for my own Christmas dinner—though I can't say I cared much for it—if I got one at all, it must be upon credit, since my drawing would not be finished for another week. Credit, of course, I would not think of. Any day in the week or year, I would rather starve than owe money. However, I was not going to cry about plum-pudding, though once or twice it made me hungry to think of the dinner in the great hall at Vaughan Park on the Christmas eve; a much more elaborate matter in the old time, than the meal served in the dining-room next day.

Now I sat in my little room this dreary Christmas eve; and do what I would, I could not help thinking a little. It was a gusty evening, cold and damp, with scuds of sleet and snow, as yet it had not made up its mind whether to freeze or thaw. Nevertheless, the streets were full of merry laughing parties, proud of their bargains for the Christmas cheer; and as they went by, the misletoe and the holly glistened in the flickering gaslight.

For old recollection's sake, I had made believe to dress my little room with some few sprigs of laurel and unberried holly; the sceptre branch, all cobbed with coral beads, was too expensive for me. Misletoe I wanted not. Who was there now to kiss me?

From the sheer craving of human nature for a word of kindness, I had called, that afternoon, upon Mrs. Elton. But good as she was and sweet to me, she had near relatives coming; and I saw or fancied, that I should be in the way. Yet I thought that her mother heart yearned toward me as she said " Good bye," and showed me out by the Christmas tree, all trembling to be lighted.

Now I sat alone and lonely by the flickering of three pennyworth of wood which I had bought recklessly, for the sake of the big ash-tree that used to glow with the lichen peeling round it on the old Christmas hearth, where I was believed the heiress. The little spark and sputter of my sallow billet (chopped by the poor old people at St. Pancras workhouse) led me back through eight sad years to the last merry time when my father was keeping his latest Christmas, and I his pride and hope was prouder than all, at being just ten years old.

How he carved and ladled the gravy; how he flourished his knife and fork with a joke all hot for every one; how he smiled when the thrice-helped farmers sent for another slice, and laughed when the crow-boy was nearly choked with plum-pudding; how he patted me on the head and caught me for a kiss, when I, dressed up as head-waitress, with my long hair all tied back, pulled his right arm and pointed to widow Hiatt's plate—the speech he made after dinner, when I was amazed at his eloquence and clapped my little hands, and the way he made me stand up on a chair and drink the Queen's health first—then the hurrahs of the tenants and servants, and how they kissed me outside—all this goes through my memory as the smoke of the billet goes up the chimney, and the tears steal under my eyelids.

Then I see the long hall afterwards, with the tables cleared away and the lights hung round the tapestry, and the yule log roaring afresh; my father (a type of the true English gentleman, not of the past but the present century), holding the hand of his wife (a lady of no condescending airs, but true womanly warmth and love)—both dressed for the tenants' ball as if for the lord-lieutenant's; both eager to lead off the country dance, and beating their feet to the music. Next them, a laughing child in a little white frock and pink slip (scarce to be known for myself), hand-in-hand with my brave chevalier, Master Roderick Blount, accounted by Cooky and both lady's-maids, and most of all by himself, my duly affianced lord.

Then the housekeeper, starched beyond measure, yet not too stiff to smile, and open for the nonce even to jokes about courtship, yielding her gracious hand for the dance to the senior tenant, a man with great calves, red face, and snow-white hair. After them come—

Hark! a loud knock and a ring. It is just in time before I begin the palinode. Who can want me to-night? I want no one but those I cannot have, whom the fire has now restored me, though the earth has hidden them.

Mrs. Shelfer is hard at work in the kitchen, preparing a wonderful supper for Charley, who has promised to come home. She has canvassed the chance of his keeping this promise fifty times in the day. Hope cries "yes;" experience whispers "no." At any rate the knock is not his, for he always carries a latch-key.

She calls up the stairs "Miss Valence!" before she goes to the door, for who knows but she might be murdered in the midst of her Christmas pudding? I come out to prove my existence and stand in the dark on the landing. She draws back the bolt; I hear a gruff voice as if it came through a hat.

"Young 'ooman by the name of Clara Waun live here?"

"Yes to be sure; Miss Valence you mean, my good friend."

"The name on this here ticket ain't Walence, but Waun."

"All right, my good friend. All right. It's just the same."

"Hor, I don't know that though. Jim, the name

of the party here ain't Waun after all. It be Walence. And three blessed days us has been all over London !"

Jim, from the top of the van, suggests that, after all, Walence and Waun be much of a muchness. For his part, he'll be blessed if he'll go any further with it. Let him and Ben look at the young lady, and see if she be like the card. Meanwhile, of course, I come forward and claim the parcel, whatever it is. Mrs. Shelfer redoubles her assurances, and calls the man a great oaf, which has more effect than anything.

" Why, Jim, this must be Charley's missus ; Charley Shelfer's missus ! Him as beat you so at skittles last week, you know."

" Ah, he did *so*. And I'd like to back him again you, Ben, for a quart all round."

This fact is decisive. Who can doubt any more ? But for all that, the book must be signed in the name of " Waun," with which of course I comply. When the two strong men have, with much difficulty (of which they made much more), lowered the enormous package from the van, Ben stands wiping his forehead. " Lor, how hot it be to-night to be sure ! And the job us has had with this big lump sure*ly !* Both the handles come off long ago. I wish my missus had got a feather-bed half the weight of that. Five-and-twenty year I've been along of this company, man and boy, but I never see such a direction as that there in all my born days. Did ever you, Jim?"

"Well," replies Jim, "I've seed a many queer ones, but none as could come up to that. And who'd a thought after all their trouble—for I'm blessed if they wrote that there under a week—who'd a' thought they'd a put 'Waun' on it when they meant 'Walence.' But the young lady is awaiting for us to drink her health, Ben, and a merry Christmas to her."

"How much is the carriage?" I ask, trembling for my change of the half-sovereign.

"Nothing, miss. Only eightpence for delivery. It be paid to Paddington, and if ever our Company airned eightpence, I'm blessed if they haven't airned it now. Thank you, Miss, and werry handsome on you, and us hopes the contents will prove to your liking, Miss, and make you a merry Christmas."

Away they go with the smoking horses, after carrying into the little kitchen the mighty maun, which Mrs. Shelfer, with my assistance, could not stir.

" Bless me, Miss Valence, what a direction ! " cries Mrs. Shelfer, when the full light falls upon it.

The direction was written in round hand upon a strip of parchment, about four inches wide and at least eight feet in length. It came from the bottom all up over the cover and down upon the other side, so that no one could open the basket without breaking it asunder. It was as follows :—

" Miss Clara Vaughan lodges at number seven in Prince Albert Street in London town near Windsor Castle in Gloucestershire the daughter of Mr. Henry Valentine Vaughan Esquire a nice tall young lady her always wears black things and walks very peart pale with a little red on her cheeks when they lets her alone can't be no mistake without it be done a purpose If so be this here little maun bain't brought to her safe and sweet and wholesome will be prosecuted with the *utmost rigour of the law* signed John Huxtable his mark × witness Timothy Badcock his'n ×."

I wondered much whether Mr. Beany Dawe had been called in to achieve this masterpiece of manuscript, which was all in large round hand, but without any stops. It seemed beyond poor Sally's art, yet there

were some loops and downstrokes that must be dear
little Sally's. I took it off with much trouble—the
parchment was joined in four places—and I have it
now.

Meanwhile Mrs. Shelfer was dancing around it,
neglecting her supper in the wonder of this gigantic
hamper. "Let me get a chopper, Miss, you'll never get
it open. Why it's sewed as tight as an oyster."

However, I did get it open at last, and never shall I
forget the contents. There was a month's food for a
family of twelve. First came hay, such as I never
smelt out of Devonshire; then eighteen rolls of butter,
each with a snowy cloth around it; the butter so golden
even at that time of year, that Mrs. Shelfer compared
it to the yolk of an egg looking out of the white.
Then a storey of clotted cream and beautiful lard and
laver, which they knew I loved. Then a floor of hay.
Below it a pair of guinea fowls, two large turkeys, and
most carefully wrapped from the rest a fine hare filled
with dried sweet herbs. Below these a flitch of bacon,
two wood-smoked hams, a pair of tongues, a leg of
Exmoor mutton, and three bottles of best elder wine.
Then a brown paper parcel containing Sally's last copy-

book (I had set her copies for half a year to come) and
a long letter, the first I had ever received from Tossil's
Barton.

When all was out at last, after the greatest delight
and laughter as each thing appeared, I fell back in
utter dismay at the spectacle before me. Mrs. Shelfer
sat on the floor unable to find her way out, she was
so flounced and tippeted with good things. When I
came to her relief, she did nothing but go round and
round what was left of the little room, humming a
Catholic hymn, and pressing both hands to her side.

But something must be done at once. Waste is
wickedness; how could we stave it off? Everything
would depend upon the weather. At present all was
beautifully fresh, thanks to the skilful packing and the
frost, albeit the mighty package had made the round
of all the Albert Streets in London. Mrs. Shelfer
would have looked at it for a month, and at intervals
exclaimed, "Bless me, my good friend, that beats
Charley's pockets. How they must eat in Devonshire!"

"Come, Mrs. Shelfer, what good are you at house-
keeping? You don't help me at all. Let us put most
of it out of doors at once. You have no cellar, and

I suppose they have none in London.   At least we can give it the chance of the open air, and it is not snowing now."

"Oh, but the cats, Miss!"

"Well, I must find some plan for them before we go to bed. Now come and help, that's a good little creature, and I'll give you some elder wine when we have done."

So we got all that was taintable into the little yard, while Tom, who never stole, except when quite sure of impunity, looked on very sagely. There we fixed it all up to the wall secure, except from cats, of whom a roving band serenaded me every night. I presented Mrs. Shelfer at once with a turkey—a specimen of natural history not found by the roadside, even on Mr. Shelfer's Sabbath journey—also a ham, and three rolls of butter. As to the rest, I would think what to do with it afterwards.

Mrs. Shelfer kept off the cats until midnight, after which I held them at bay by the following means. With one of my mineral paints mingled with some phosphorus, I drew upon a black board a ferocious terrier, the size of life, with fangs unsheathed, bristles

erect, and eyes starting out of his head. We tried the
effect in the dark on poor Tom, who arched his back,
and sputtered with the strongest execration, then turned
and fled ignobly, amid roars of laughter from Mr.
Shelfer, who by this time was come home. This one-
headed Cerberus being hung so as to oscillate in the
wind, right across the cat-leap, I felt quite safe, so long
as my chemical mixture should continue luminous.

CHAPTER XV.

Dear little Sally's letter gave me the greatest delight. It was all in round hand, and had taken at least a week to write, and she must have washed her hands almost every time. There were no stops in it, but I have put some. The spelling was wonderfully good for her, but here and there I have shaped it to the present fashion.

"Please Miss Clara dear, father and mother and I begs their most respectable duty and love and they hopes no offence and will you be so kind as to have this here little hamper and wishes it was ten times as much but hopes you will excuse it and please to eat it all yourself Miss. All the pegmate be our own doctrine, and very wholesome, and we have took all the hair off, please Miss, because you said one time you didn't like it. Likely you'll remember, Miss, the young black sow as twisted her tail to the left, her as Tim was ringing the day as I wrote first copy, and the other chillers ran out, well most of it be she, Miss. Father say as he don't think they ever see butter in London town, but Beany Dawe says yes for they makes a plenty out of red herrings and train oil.

Please Miss, Tabby Badcock would go on the ice in the old saw-pit last Sunday, by the upper linhay when I told her it would not bear, and so her fell through and would have been drownded at last, only our little Jack crawled over the postesses and give her his heel to hold on by, and please Miss it would have done your heart good, mother says, to see how Tim Badcock dressed her when he come home from church for getting her best frock all of a muck.

Please Miss, Beany Dawe come when you was gone, and made a poem about you, and father like it so much he give him free of the cider and as he was going home he fell into a bit of a ditch down Breakneck hill, and when he come to himself the road had taken to run the wrong way Beany don't know how for the life of him, so he come back here 'nolus wolus' he saith and that be the way to spell it and no mistake, and here he have been ever since a-making of poems and sawing up hellums out of the lower cleeve, and he sleepth in

the onion loft and Suke can't have no rest of nights
for the noise he makes making verses. Mother tell
Suke to pote him down stairs and too good for him,
but father say no, he be a fine chap for sure and airneth
his meat and drink, let alone all the poetry.

Please Miss he wanted to larn me to write, but
father say no I had got better learning than hisn, and
I say he may learn Tabby Badcock if he will, but he
shan't learn me.   No tino."

How she tossed her pretty curls when she wrote this
I'll be bound.   I wished that I could see her.

" Please Miss I be forced to write this when he be
away, or he'd a made it all in poetry ; and Tim Badcock
tell me to be sure to tell you as how at the wrastling
to Barnstaple fair, week after you was gone, father was
so crule unkid that in playing off the ties he heaved
a Cornisher up through the chandelier, and a come
down with a candle stuck so fast down his throat doctor
was forced to set it a-fire and blow with a pair of
bellises afore he could put him to rights. Cornisher
be all right again now, Tim saith, but he have a made
up his mind not to wrastle no more in Devonshire.

Please Miss, father saith before this here goes he'll

shoot the old hare as sits in the top of the cleeve if Queen Victoria transports him for it with hard labour. Tim have made four pops at her, but he say the powder were crooked.

Please Miss Clara, all the eggs as my little black hen have laid, since the last of the barley was housed, is to be sewed up inside the Turkey with the black comb; he be strutting about in the court and looking at me now as peart as a gladdy; but her have not laid more than a dozen to now, though I have been up and whistled to her in the tallat every morning and evening same as we used to do when you was in good spirits. But the other hens has not laid none at all.

Please Miss, father say as how he have sold such a many beasties, he be afeared to keep all the money in the house, and he have told mother to sew up the rent for next Ladyday in the turkey with the white comb when he be killed and he humbly hope no offence.

Please Miss Clara, us has had three letters from you, and I reads them all to father and mother every Sunday evening, and Joe the Queen's boy don't know but what he lost another one in leathering the jackass across the brook after the rain. Joe tells as he can't say for certain, because why he baint no scholar the same as us be, and Joe only knows the letters by the pins they sticks in his sleeve afore he leaves Martinhoe. Whoever 'twas for he thinks there was crockery in it by reason it sunk so quick. Anyhow mother give him a little tap with a mop on the side of his head, to make him mind the Queen's business, and didn't he holler a bit, and he flung down the parson's letters all in the muck, but us washed them in a bucket and let parson have them on Sunday. Joe Queen's boy haven't been nigh us since, and they did say to Martinhoe us shouldn't have no more letters, but father say if he don't he will show the man there what a forehip mean pretty smart.

Please Miss Clara, us would have written afore, but mother say no, not till I finish twelve copybooks one every week, that the folks to London town might see the way as they ought to write and spell. Father say London be in Gloucestershire, but I am most sure it baint, and Beany Dawe shake his head and won't tell, and mother believe he don't know.

Please Miss, there be a new babby come a month agone and better, and mother find out as how it be a girl, and please if you have no objection Miss, and if you don't think as it would be a liberty, us has all made up our minds upon having it christened Clara, and please to say Miss if it be too high, or any way unfitty. Father be 'most afeared that it sound too grand for the like of us, but mother says as the Huxtables was thought brave things on, to Coom and Parracombe a hundred years agone.

Please Miss, father heard to Coom market last week, as there's going to be a French invasion, and they be sure to go to London first, and he beg you to let him know as soon as ever there be one, and he come up at once with the big ash-stick and the ivy on it as growed in Challacombe wood, and see as they doesn't hurt you, Miss.

Please Miss, the young chap as saved you from the great goyal come here to ask for you, day after you was gone, and mother believes he baint after no good, by token he would not come in nor drink a drop of cider.

Please Miss, father say it make his heart ache every night, to think of you all to yourself in the wicked London town, and he go down the lane to the white gate every evening in the hope to see you acoming, and mother say if you be a selling red and blue picturs her hope you will send for they as father gave the hog's puddens for, and us wont miss them at all.

And Miss Clara dear, I expect you'll be mazed to see how I writes and spells, father say it must be in the family, and I won't write no more till I have finished another dozen of copy books; and oh dear how I do wish that you were come back again, but father say to me to say no more about it for fear to make you cry, Miss. All the little childers except the new babby who have not seen you yet, sends their hearts' loves and duty and a hundred kisses, and father and mother the same, and Timothy Badcock, and Tabby, and Suke, and Beany Dawe, now he knows it.

I remain, Miss Clara dear, your thankful and loving scholar to command,

SARAH HUXTABLE.

Signed all this here papper scrawl in the settle by the fire.

JOHN HUXTABLE his mark ×
HONOR HUXTABLE hern ×."

CHAPTER XVI.

I WAS much grieved at the loss of my last letter to Tossil's Barton, because it contained my little Christmas presents for all the family. It was registered for security, but I suppose they "took no count" of that where the delivery of letters depended so much upon luck. Of their Christmas present to me I resolved to give the surplus to those who would be the better for it, and not (according to the usual law of such things) to those who did not want it, and would make return with interest. So on the Christmas morning Mrs. Shelfer and myself, each carrying a large basket, went to the mews round the corner, and distributed among the poor lodgers there, more Christmas dinners than had ever entered those doors before; and how grateful the poor things were, only they all wanted the best.

Now the school of design was closed for a while, and

I worked hard for several days at the landscape for Mr. Oxgall, though the store of provisions sent me and the rent enclosed in the turkey had saved me from present necessity.

On the day of all days in the year the saddest and darkest to me, I could not keep to my task, but went for a change of thoughts to the school, now open again.

It was the 30th of December, 1850, and, though I crouch not to the mumming of prigs scolloped out at the throat, who block out with a patchwork screen the simple hearth of religion, and kneel at an ashbin to warm themselves; though I don't care a herring for small anniversaries dotted all over the calendar, and made by some Murphy of old; yet I reverence deeply the true feasts of Church and Chapel, the refreshings of faith and charity, whereupon we forgive and are sorry for those who work hard to mar them. Neither does it seem to me—so far as my timid and wavering judgment extends—to be superstition or vanity, if we dare to set mark by those dates in our own little span which God has scarred on our memory.

In the long dark room so bare and comfortless, and,

to-day, so lonely and cold, I got my usual books and studies, and tried, all in vain, to fix my attention on them. Finding the effort so fruitless, I packed up my things in the little black bag and rose to depart. Turning round, I saw on the table, where students' works were exhibited, a small object newly placed there. It was a statuette in white marble of a magnificent red deer, such as I had seen once or twice in the north of Devon. The listening attitude, the turn of the neck, the light poise of the massive head, even the mild, yet spirited eye, and the quivering sensitive lip, I could answer for them all, they were done to the very life. Truth, power, and elegance triumphed in every vein of it. For a minute I stood overcome with wonder. If this were the work of a youthful sculptor, England might hope at last for something beyond the grotesque.

Before me rose at once all the woodland scenery, the hill-side garbed with every shade of green, the brambled quarry standing forth, the trees, the winding vales embosoming the light, the haze that hovers above the watersmeet, bold crests of amaranth heath behind, and far away the russet wold of Exmoor. The stag in the

foreground of my landscape, I feel so grateful to him
for this expanse of vision that I stoop down and kiss
him, while no one can see me. As I bend, the gordit
drops from its warm home in my breast. By some
impulse undefined I lift the ribbon from my neck, and
hang the little fairy's heart on the antlers of the Devonshire deer. Out springs from behind a chest full of
casts and models—what model can compare with her?
—the loveliest of all lovely beings, my little Isola
Ross.

I hide the tears in my eyes, and try to look cold
and reserved. What use is it? One smile of hers
would have disarmed Belial.

"It isn't my fault, dear. It isn't indeed. Oh, please
give me that cordetto. No don't. That is why I
loved you so at first sight. And here is all my money
dear. I have carried it about ever since, though I
sewed up the purse not to spend it, and only once
cut it open. They made me promise, and I would
not eat for three days, and I tried to be sulky with
Pappy because he did not care; they made me promise
with all my honour not to go and see you, and Cora
came about with me so that I had no chance of

breaking it. And I would not tell them where you lived, dear; but I led old Cora a dance through your street on the side you live, till she began to suspect. But I could never see you, though I looked in at all the windows till I was quite ashamed, and the people kissed their hands to me."

Poor little dear! I lived upstairs, and could not have seen her without standing out on the balcony, which was about the size of a chess-board. If she had not been so simple as to walk on my side of the street, she must have seen me ere long, for I sat all day near the window to draw, when I was not away at my school.

I forgave her most graciously for having done me no wrong, and kissed her with all my heart. Her breath was as sweet as violets in Spring clover, and her lips warm and soft as a wren's nest. On receiving my forgiveness, away she went dancing down the long room, with her cloak thrown off, and her hair tossing all out of braid, and her exquisite buoyant figure floating as if on a cloud. Of course there was no one there, or even impulsive Isola would hardly have taken her frolic; and yet I am not sure. She never thought harm of any one, and never imagined that any one could think harm of her.

After a dozen flits of some rapid elegant dance quite unknown to me (who have never had much of dancing), but which I supposed to be Scotch, back she came out of breath, and kissed me ever so many times, and kissed my gordit too, and told me never to part with it. One thing she was sure of, that her Papa could not resist me now, and when he was told of it I should come to their house the next day. And she knew I was dreadfully proud, but would I, for her sake, forgive her Pappy? . Of course, he knew nothing about me, and she had never told him my name, though she could not help telling my story, at least all she knew of it; but he was so dreadfully jealous of her, he did not want any one to have a touch of her glove but himself.

Looking at her pure sweet face, I could well believe it; but how could he bear to see that dear little thing go three days without food? Most likely she had exaggerated. Although she was truthful as light, sometimes her quick fancy and warmth, like the sun-shine itself, would bring out some points too strongly.

However, I was prepared, without that, to dislike the Professor, for, as a general rule, I don't like men who moralise; at least if their philosophy is frigid. Nevertheless, I promised very readily to forgive her Papa, for I did so love that Isola. Her nature was so different to mine, so light and airy, elastic and soft; in short (if I must forsake my language), the complement of my own. We chatted, or rather she did, for at least half an hour; and then she told me old Cora was coming to fetch her at three o'clock. Once more I rose to depart, for I feared she might get into trouble, if the old nurse should find her so intimate with a stranger.

But Isola told me that she did not care for her a bit, and she had quite set her heart on my meeting her brother Conrad, the sculptor of that magnificent stag. Perhaps he would come with Cora, but he was so altered now, she could never tell what he would do. Since the time she first saw me, Conrad had come of age, and she could not guess what it was all about, but there had been a dreadful disturbance between him and his father, and he had actually gone to live away from the family. She thought it must be about money, or some such nasty thing; but even Cora did not know, or if she did, the old thing would not tell. It had made poor Isola cry till her eyes were sore, but now she supposed she must make up her mind to it all. But she would tell the truth, she did hate being treated like a baby when she was a full-grown woman; how much taller did they expect her to be? And what was much worse, she did want so to comfort them both, and how could she do it without knowing what was the matter? It was too bad, and she wished she was a boy, with all her heart she did.

She went on talking like this till her gentle breast fluttered, and her coral lips quivered, and the tears stole down her long lashes, and she crept to me closer for comfort.

I was clasping her round little waist, and kissing the bright drops away, when in burst a dark, scraggy woman, who must, of course, be old Cora. She tore the poor child from my arms, and scowled at me fiercely enough to frighten a girl unacquainted with real terrors.

I met her dark gaze with a calm contempt, beneath which it quailed and fell. She mumbled some words in a language or *patois*, which I supposed to be Gaelic, and led off her charge towards the door.

She had mistaken her adversary. Was I to be pushed aside, like a gingerbread woman tempting a weak-stomached child? I passed them; then turned and confronted the hag.

"Have the goodness, old woman, to walk behind this young lady and me. When we want your society, we will ask for it. Isola Ross, come with me, unless you prefer a rude menial's tyranny to a lady's affection."

Isola was too frightened to speak. I know not what would have been the result, if the old hag, who was glaring about, rather taken aback, but still clutching that delicate arm, had not suddenly spied my fairy's heart, as yet unrestored to its sanctuary.

She stared, for a moment, in wide amazement; then her whole demeanour was altered. She cringed, and fawned, and curtseyed, as if I had worn a tiara. She dropped my dear Isola's arm, and fell behind like a negress. My poor little pet was trembling and cold with fright, for (as she told me afterwards) she had never seen old Cora in such a passion before, and the superstitious darling dreaded the evil eye.

As we went towards Isola's home, I could not help thinking how fine the interview would be between Mrs. Shelfer and Cora, if I only chose to carry that vanquished beldame thither; but sage discretion (was I not now eighteen?), and the thought of that solemn day prevented me. So I took them straight home, leading Isola while she guided me, and turning sometimes, with complacency, to encourage old Cora behind us.

The house they lived in was a high but narrow one, dull-looking and dark, with area rails in front. Some little maiden came to the door, and I took my leave on the steps. Dear Isola, now in high spirits again, kissed me, like a peach quite warm in the sun, and promised to come the next day, about which there could now be no difficulty.

Old Cora bent low as she wished me good evening and begged leave to kiss my cordetto. This I granted, but took good care not to let it pass out of my hands; she admired it so much, especially when allowed to examine it, and there was such a greedy light in her eyes, that I was quite sure she would steal it upon the first chance; and therefore I went straightway and bought a guard of thick silk cord, as a substitute for the black riband, which was getting worn.

' And so I came home before dark, full of wonder, but feeling rather triumphant, and greatly delighted at having recovered dear Isola.

END OF VOL. I.

LONDON:
R. CLAY, SON, AND TAYLOR, PRINTERS,
BREAD STREET HILL.

9 783337 149536